*Her hand ~~hovered~~ ~~over~~ ~~the~~
phone receiver as she worked
up the courage to dial.*

If Vince were to catch her, she would be dead
for sure. Once again she cursed herself for not
realizing sooner the kind of man he was. She'd
been seduced by his expensive car and thick
wallet—by his power.

She fingered the two-karat diamond studs in
her lobes. She had a case full of precious gems,
a closet full of designer clothes—and for what?
By the time she'd begun to suspect who Vince
really was, what he'd done, it was too late. She
was in too deep. He owned her.

She had to do the right thing. Before she could
talk herself out of it, she picked up the receiver,
dropped in two quarters and dialed. It rang four
times before someone answered in a gruff voice,
"FBI."

She had to do it. It was the *right* thing to do.
"I want to report a murder."

Dear Reader,

What a glorious time of year—full of shopping, holiday cheer and endless opportunities to eat baked goods. For your shopping list I suggest this month's stellar lineup of Silhouette Intimate Moments books—romances with adrenaline.

New York Times bestselling author Maggie Shayne delights readers with *Feels Like Home* (#1395), an emotional tale from her miniseries THE OKLAHOMA ALL-GIRL BRANDS, in which a cop returns to his hometown and falls for a woman from his past. Will a deadly threat end their relationship? In Maggie Price's *Most Wanted Woman* (#1396), from her miniseries LINE OF DUTY, a police sergeant is intrigued by a bartender with a dark secret and an irresistible face. Don't miss it!

You'll love Karen Whiddon's next story, *Secrets of the Wolf* (#1397), from her spine-tingling miniseries THE PACK. Here, a determined heroine seeks answers about her past, which leads her to a handsome sheriff with his own secrets. Can she trust this mysterious man and the passion that consumes them? Michelle Celmer's story is *Out of Sight* (#1398), a thrilling tale in which an embittered FBI agent searches for a missing witness and finds her…in his bed. Will she flee before helping bring a killer to justice?

So, take a break from the nonstop festivities and get engrossed in these fabulous love stories. Happy reading!

Sincerely,

Patience Smith
Associate Senior Editor
Silhouette Intimate Moments

Please address questions and book requests to:
Silhouette Reader Service
U.S.: 3010 Walden Ave., P.O. Box 1325, Buffalo, NY 14269
Canadian: P.O. Box 609, Fort Erie, Ont. L2A 5X3

MICHELLE CELMER

Out of Sight

INTIMATE MOMENTS™

Published by Silhouette Books

America's Publisher of Contemporary Romance

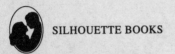 **SILHOUETTE BOOKS**

ISBN 0-373-27468-8

OUT OF SIGHT

Visit Silhouette Books at www.eHarlequin.com

Printed in U.S.A.

MICHELLE CELMER

Bestselling author lives in southeastern Michigan with her husband, their three children, two dogs and two cats. When she's not writing or busy being a mom, you can find her in the garden or curled up with a romance novel. And if you twist her arm real hard you can usually persuade her into a day of power shopping.

Michelle loves to hear from readers. Visit her Web site at: www.michellecelmer.com, or write her at P.O. Box 300, Clawson, MI 48017.

To my grandma Irene, my most loyal fan.

Prologue

"Time to go, Gantz." Special Agent Will Bishop hoisted his prisoner up by the arm from the motel room chair. "You've got a date in court."

"They ain't gonna let me testify," Gantz said. Sweat dripped from the man's meaty face and soaked through his Italian silk suit. A suit that probably cost him more than Will made in a month. "I'll be dead before I get to the courthouse."

"You're breaking my heart." Ryan Thomas opened the door, letting in a blast of hot, humid air and early-morning sunshine. He signaled to the men standing guard around the perimeter of the lot.

It wasn't often Will got to work with Ryan these days, but with his regular partner still out on maternity leave, they were paired for this case. It had made the long shifts in this sleazy little motel guarding Gantz easier to stomach. But he was glad it was finally over. His wife was really nagging him about the long hours he'd been working. Which meant she'd been nagging him only slightly more than usual.

"Looks clear," Ryan said.

"Time to roll." Will cuffed Gantz and shoved him toward the door. "Let's go."

"I'm telling you, man. The family ain't gonna let it happen. And don't think they'll stop at me. You guys are as good as dead."

Ryan held the door open. "There are five agents in that parking lot. If someone was out there waiting for you, we would know."

"What are you worried about Gantz? In a week you'll have a new face and a new identity," Will said, unable to mask the disgust in his voice. Lou Gantz, a hit man responsible for the deaths of at least thirty men—many of whom had been waiting to testify in court—was getting a walk in exchange for his testimony against the Sardoni family, New York's most vicious organized-crime organization. Until now, nearly every member of the family had managed to avoid prosecution. Witnesses either recanted their claims, were found floating in the river or simply disappeared without a trace.

Not this time. The family's top associates were under indictment, and the bureau had taken every possible precaution to keep Gantz's location secure.

This time they were going down.

"Move it." Will gave him another shove, out the door into the parking lot.

Full-fledged panic crept into the man's tone. "I'm tellin' ya, we're all dead."

Ryan opened the sedan door and heaved Gantz in the back, then turned to Will. "Call and let them know we're on the way."

Will reached in his jacket pocket, but it was empty. "Hell, I left my phone in the room."

"What's with you and that phone?"

Will shrugged. He was always forgetting the damned thing.

"I think it's subconscious. I think you forget it so you don't have to talk to your wife."

He laughed. "Yeah, could be."

His current wife—bride number two—called him constantly. She was making roast for dinner, was that okay or would he prefer chicken—he would be home for dinner, right? Or she saw a dress on sale in the weekend paper that she'd like to buy, did he mind? And by the way, the mechanic said it would cost an extra fifty dollars to fix the car, should she tell him that was all right?

It was as if she couldn't make a single decision without first consulting him. Sometimes he wondered if he would have been better off staying single. Of course, if he divorced her, he would be paying alimony to *two* ex-wives. Between that and legal fees, it was probably cheaper to stay married—and miserable.

Ryan on the other hand had one of those perfect marriages that made even the hardest of characters ripe with envy. He had a gorgeous, supportive wife, three beautiful children. Five years more and he would be retiring from the bureau.

He had the kind of life Will had always wished for. Yet somehow Will kept ending up with clingy, dependent, whiny women. They had yet to hit their first anniversary and already his second marriage had begun to feel like a heavy chain around his shoulders, dragging him down.

"Hurry up, we're gonna be late," Ryan said and slipped into the driver's seat.

Will shouldered his way back through the hotel room door, spotting his phone on the table next to the window. As he reached for it, he heard the car start. Then there was a flash and an earsplitting rumble. The window imploded and he was flung back against the bed. Too late he threw up his arm to shield himself from the blast, screaming in pain as shards of glass and debris tore into the left side of his face. For a second he sat there, stunned. What remained of the curtains hung smoldering in the window, and thick black smoke belched in from the parking lot. Then the reality of what had happened hit him square in the chest.

Car bomb. And Ryan had been inside.

Noxious black smoke filled the room, gagging him, and through the ringing in his ears he heard people shouting. He slid to the floor, where the air wasn't so thick, trying to get his bearings. Keeping his body low to the ground, he crawled toward the dim light coming through the open door. Pulling himself up in the door frame, he staggered out of the room and turned to see the car. His knees buckled and he went down hard on the blacktop.

It was completely engulfed in flames.

Las Vegas, one week later

Crystal's hand trembled on the pay-phone receiver as she worked up the courage to dial. She'd committed to memory the number for the New York office. If Vince were to catch her with the number on her, she would be dead for sure.

Once again she cursed herself for not realizing sooner the kind of man Vince was. She'd been seduced by his expensive car and thick wallet—by his power. And sure, she'd had a pretty good idea that wherever that money and power had come from, it probably wasn't legal. It wouldn't be the first time she'd dated a guy that preferred to keep his business dealings under the radar. Hell, this was Vegas. It was all a part of the charm, the excitement.

She fingered the two-carat diamond studs in her lobes. She had a case full of precious gems, a closet full of designer clothes, and for what? By the time she'd begun to suspect who Vince really was, begun to put it all together, it was too late. She was in too deep. He owned her.

When she'd overheard him talking about a package being delivered and heard Gantz's name, then later found the duffel bag full of money in his office closet—more money than she'd seen in her whole life—her worst fears had been confirmed.

Vince was a hit man.

Not only had Gantz been killed, but an FBI agent

had been in the car with him. A family man. When
Crystal had seen the agent's wife on the news, three
young children clinging to her side, something inside
her had snapped. She'd decided right then, for the first
time in her life she had to do the right thing. Even if
that meant they would get her, too, just as they had gotten Gantz. She had to take that chance. She would
never be able to live with herself otherwise. Even
though most of the people Vince took out were scum,
they were still people. They had wives and children
who loved them.

It had to end here.

Before she could talk herself out of it, she picked
up the receiver and dropped two quarters into the
phone. With trembling fingers, she dialed. It rang four
times before someone answered in a gruff voice, "FBI."

She clutched a hand to her sequin-covered bosom,
feeling as if her heart might beat clear through her sur-
gically enhanced chest. She had to do it. It was the *right*
thing to do. "I want to report a murder."

Chapter 1

Present Day, New York

Will tossed a manila folder on Dale Robbins's desk. "I think I found her."

The assistant director set down his pen and gazed up at Will, a look of barely contained annoyance on his face. "Found who?"

"Crystal."

"Jesus, not Gantz again." Robbins opened the file and scanned its contents, then shoved it back across the desk. "You're talking about a four-year-old closed case. You know as well as I do that Crystal is probably buried in the desert somewhere. Give it up already."

He wished he could, but finding Crystal had become an obsession. She was the last one who could testify against Ryan's killer. By the time they'd discovered who the leak was—the man in the bureau responsible for giving away the location of the hotel where they were holding Gantz—he'd been floating in the East River.

If it was the last thing he did, Will would bring Vince Collucci to justice. He owed it to Ryan's family. "Hear me out. This time I think I've really got something."

His superior leaned back in his chair and folded his arms over his chest. "You have two minutes."

"Remember the girl we were watching right after Crystal? Stephanie Fair?"

"The Vegas showgirl?"

"That's the one. Because of her connection to the Sardoni family, she's still on the hot list. She got a call the other day from Colorado."

Robbins shrugged as if to say, *Yeah, so?*

"As far as we know, she doesn't have any ties there. So I traced it. The call originated from a divorce retreat outside of Denver. A place called Healing Hearts."

"So what? Maybe she's got a friend staying there."

"Highly unlikely considering the class of people she associates with. It's an upscale place. I did some digging and found something interesting. The retreat was started a little over three years ago, just months after Crystal disappeared with Vince's money. The owner is some sort of recluse, rarely shows her face, so I ran her name."

Robbins sat a little taller in his chair. "I'm listening."

"It's a fake. The retreat is owned by some private corporation. Unfortunately that's all I was able to find out."

"So what do you want from me?"

"I want you to put me in undercover."

Robbins shook his head. "I know you want to solve this one, Will, but the director is not going to go for this. I'm going to need more. If you can get a positive ID—"

"Sir, I know it's her."

"Get me some proof."

Will took a deep breath, shoving back the frustration rising up inside him. "I've done all I can from here. I've hit a dead end."

"You know, even if you do find her, you can't force her to testify. If she wouldn't before, you can be sure she won't now."

"If I charge her with accessory she will, if she's faced with life in prison. She took the hit money. We have no idea the extent of her involvement."

"We *think* she took the money."

"Why else was Vince so hot to find her after she disappeared?"

"Even if she did, charging her with accessory is a stretch. And besides, how are you going to know if it's her? The pictures we've got from the surveillance tapes are grainy as hell. Not to mention, she's probably changed her appearance."

"She does have one distinguishing mark—a heart-shaped birthmark high up on her inner thigh. The information supposedly came from Vince himself. So if I find the birthmark, I find the girl."

"I don't even want to ask how you plan to see it."

"I'm hoping I won't have to." He leaned both hands on the desk, feeling desperate. For the first time in four years he knew he was close. He could solve this. He *had* to solve it so he could close his eyes and not see the vision of Ryan's charred remains slumped over the steering wheel. So he could look Ryan's wife and children in the eye and no longer feel as though he'd failed them. "You have to let me try."

Robbins shook his head. "I'm sorry, Will, but I can't sanction an operation of this magnitude without proof."

He'd gone into this knowing it was a long shot. The truth was, he'd expected as much, and like any good agent, he had a backup plan. "Then I respectfully request a four-week leave of absence."

"For…?"

"It's no secret my last divorce was messy. No one will question my need to take a month off for a trip to Healing Hearts. The next session begins in two weeks."

Robbins laughed. "I'm not denying you could use some headshrinking, Bishop, but *you* at a divorce retreat? I just don't see it. Besides, this place must cost a fortune."

"I've got some money stashed away, stocks I can cash in. I want to do this. I *have* to, for Ryan's family. They need closure."

"They need closure or you do?"

They both knew the answer to that.

Robbins sat back in his chair, letting out a long breath. "Look, if this is something you need to do, I can't stop you. But if you find yourself in hot water,

I'm not going to be there to drag you out. You do this, you're on your own. Understood?"

"Understood. Although…"

"Although, what?"

"The retreat has a fairly vigorous screening policy. They can't know I'm with the bureau."

Robbins sighed. "Anything else?"

"Nope."

Robbins studied him for a moment, as if he were weighing his options. Will would resign before he let anyone stop him from solving this case, and he was pretty sure the assistant director knew that. Despite being mildly belligerent and slightly obsessive at times, Will was a one hell of a good agent—one of the best in the New York office. They wouldn't want to lose him.

"Okay," he finally said. "You've got your four weeks. But if anyone asks, we never had this conversation."

"Divorce impacts every family member. It is a death of sorts. It affects self-identity, financial security and lifestyle. Here at Healing Hearts, we're dedicated to guiding families though this difficult, devastating time…."

Abi Sullivan stood in her boss's office watching through the two-way mirror into the common area as Eve, the in-house psychologist, gave her opening speech to the retreat guests—forty in total, half of whom were children. As children's activities director, she would know them all by name by week's end. She

studied their faces, memorized them. Some looked inexplicably sad, others angry and bitter, while some just
looked lost.

One boy in particular, Eric Stillson, caught her attention. He looked to be sixteen or seventeen and sat
off by himself near the back of the room. Unlike the
others, he looked bored, indifferent, as if he felt nothing at all—a pretty good indication he was tortured on
the inside. She would know. It was like looking at a
mirror image of herself half a lifetime ago.

She knew without even meeting him he would be
her special project. There was one in every group.

She turned to her employer. "So his mother just
dropped him off and left?"

"It wasn't even the mother that brought him. It was
one of their staff. A butler or something. Scary-look-
ing guy." Maureen Kelly, founder of the resort, sat at
her massive mahogany desk, a stack of files in front of
her. "So much for the concept of family counseling,
huh?"

"And I suppose his parents expect him to be *fixed*
by the time he leaves here."

Maureen gave her a rueful smile. "Don't they all?"

Abi walked over to the open picture window. In the
distance, white-tipped mountains kissed a cloudless
blue sky, and at their base Lake Cillito shimmered in
the morning sunlight. East of the sprawling main building, guest cabins dotted the landscape, and to the west
was the employee lodging where her own cabin was located.

She breathed in the clean mountain air, a feeling of

peace washing over her. She could be having the worst day in her life and needed only to look at that view to remind herself how lucky she was to be there. She would never know if it was chance or divine intervention that had caused her and Maureen to cross paths. All she did know was that in her thirty years she'd never been more happy or content. She'd found her calling—taking all the rotten experiences from her miserable childhood and using the knowledge she'd gained to help others. And she'd found a kindred spirit in Maureen.

For the first time in her life she didn't feel as if she were waiting for the other shoe to fall.

In the other room she heard Eve winding down, Abi's cue to prepare to meet the kids and introduce them to the program. For the next four weeks their days would be filled with horseback riding, hiking and swimming, crafts and scavenger hunts and of course family and individual counseling.

"Time to meet the kids," she said.

"How about dinner in my quarters Thursday night?" Maureen asked. "I'd like to go over a few new ideas for the next session." Unlike her staff, Maureen didn't share dinner with her guests in the main dining room. In fact, it was rare that she ever showed her face. She spent most of her time in her office or private living quarters.

"Should I find someone to watch Adam?" Abi asked.

"No, bring him. He can watch Nickelodeon."

"He'll love that." Since Maureen's television was

the only one at the resort with a satellite dish and local channels were limited, it was a rare treat for her son. He wouldn't make a peep.

"Six o'clock?"

"Sounds good, I'll see you then."

She buzzed Abi out of her private office and into the main office next door, where Maureen's secretary, Susie, took care of the everyday business.

"I apologize, Mr. Bishop, but that just won't be possible," Susie was saying to the man standing opposite her desk.

Looming over it was more like it. He stood at least six feet tall and, in low-riding khaki shorts and a T-shirt, had the lean muscled look of a man half his age. She was guessing, from the gray peppering the thick dark hair at his temples and the lines bracketing his eyes and mouth, he had to be pushing forty.

And handsome. Wow. He was what some of the younger female staff members would refer to as a "hottie." His face was long and lean, his cheekbones high, his eyes deep set and intense. She could see he was the Sean Connery type, the sort of man who would only improve with age. Then he turned toward her and she had to fight not to gasp. Deep scars marred the entire left half of his face.

His eyes quickly roamed over her from head to toe and back again. The move was so deliberate, so…*calculated,* she didn't know if she should feel flattered or violated.

"Ms. Kelly?" he asked in a deep and smooth voice.

Abi's defenses instantly went on alert. Running interference for Maureen was a regular part of the job, and she took it very seriously. Without Maureen, who knew where she would be? "My name is Abigale Sullivan, children's activities director. Mr. Bishop, is it?"

"Will," he said, holding out a hand for her to shake. His grip was firm and confident, his smile warm and engaging. If his appearance bothered him in the least, he didn't let it show. And oddly enough, it didn't detract from his good looks. She found herself instinctively standing a little taller, running a hand through her drab brown, pin-straight hair.

Ugh! She was *preening?* Where had that come from? It had been an awfully long time since she'd worried about using her looks to impress a man. Since she'd had Adam, she hadn't even tried. She had neither the time, the will, nor the opportunity. If nothing else, she went out of her way to make herself as invisible as possible. Since her first encounter with a boy in the backseat of a beat-up Nova, she'd had enough experience with men to last three lifetimes. All that mattered now was being a good mother to her son.

But something about the direct way this man looked at her both intrigued and disturbed her.

"Is there something I can help you with?" she asked, locking her hands behind her back to stop herself from fidgeting.

"He was asking to see Maureen," Susie said, a wary look in her eyes. She was always suspicious of people wanting to see Maureen, as if they might somehow know who she really was. Most of the staff didn't know her true identity. Only those who could be trusted were allowed into the fold, and even then only so much information was divulged.

Abi had been with her from the start and knew what Maureen stood to lose should her real identity ever be discovered.

"Is there a problem I can help you with?" Abi asked.

"No," he said. "No problem. I just wanted to thank Ms. Kelly for getting me in on such short notice. My work schedule affords me very little time for personal travel."

"As Susie said, Maureen doesn't see guests, but I'll be sure to pass along the message."

Another warm smile. "I'd appreciate that."

"Susie, Adam and I will be having dinner with Maureen Thursday night. Let the chef know, please."

"Sure thing, Abi." Susie gave Mr. Bishop one last suspicious look before she picked up the phone and dialed the extension for the kitchen.

"It was a pleasure to meet you, Mr. Bishop," Abi said and started for the door. "If you need anything else, any member of the staff can help you."

"Call me Will," he said, falling in step beside her. "You said you're the children's activities director?"

"That's right. Do you have children?"

"Unfortunately no. Or fortunately, depending on how you look at it. Both my divorces were pretty nasty. It would have been a shame to drag a child through that."

Well, he was conscientious—or that was what he wanted her to believe. Not that she had any reason to suspect he would try to deceive her, but old habits died hard. She was only now learning to trust again, to believe not everyone had ulterior motives.

They walked out into the common area. The main building as well as the smaller cabins were constructed entirely of logs, and their furnishings—knotted pine or Early American—reflected the same rustic theme. A former dude ranch, the atmosphere was much more laid-back than your average upscale resort. It didn't put on airs, and for Abi, that was its charm.

The meeting had ended and some of the guests had broken off into small groups while others left to explore the grounds. The children's orientation was scheduled to start in ten minutes, and the official activities kick-off began that night at dusk, when everyone gathered on the beach for a bonfire.

"Well," she said, turning to Mr. Bishop. "I have a lot of work to do. It was a pleasure meeting you."

He smiled and shook her hand, gripping it firmly and holding on just a fraction of a second longer than she deemed appropriate.

"The pleasure is all mine," he said. "I'm sure we'll be running into each other again."

There was something about him that bothered her, she realized as she headed for the children's activities center. Not that he'd been rude or unfriendly. Maybe it was that he'd been *too* friendly. Or maybe it was the distinct skip of her heart when he smiled at her.

Even if he did find her attractive—which she found pretty hard to swallow in the first place—a divorce retreat was certainly not the place to pick up men. There were strict rules forbidding the staff from becoming romantically involved with the guests. Likewise, the guests were discouraged from forming intimate relationships with each other. Not that it didn't occasionally occur.

As she pulled open the door, a feeling, something like a warm shiver, danced its way up the length of her spine, and she looked back in the direction from which she'd come. Mr. Bishop stood right where she'd left him, hands tucked in his shorts pockets, leaning casually against the wall.

And he was watching her.

Will saw Abi glance his way, give him a funny look, then disappear out the door. She was about as plain as they came—her drab brown hair hung straight and limp around a heart-shaped face completely devoid of makeup. Her shorts were baggy, her red faculty T-shirt oversize, hiding whatever figure she had—which, from what he could see, wasn't much. She wasn't unattractive, just…nondescript. And about as timid as a mouse. But there was something about her eyes—something remarkable. They were plain old brown and a little on the large side, which at first had given her a look of youthful innocence. Until he looked deeper and realized she could have been a hundred years old for all the wisdom and experience he saw lurking there.

He also saw distrust.

But, if she was having dinner with the owner, they must be friends. Though it would be hard-won, gaining her friendship—gaining her trust—might be the key to meeting to the elusive Maureen Kelly. And for that he would go to any lengths. Even if that meant deceiving a woman who, if the pain buried deep in her eyes was any indication, had clearly been deceived before.

Chapter 2

Abi sat alone at a table in the dining room that evening, picking at her dinner. Though she had planned to eat in her cabin with Adam, she'd wanted a chance to observe Eric. As she'd expected, he hadn't said a word during orientation and had begrudgingly participated in as few activities as he could get away with today. He hadn't made any effort to meet the other kids and now he sat by himself at the rear of the dining room. He was so alone, her heart ached for him. And as badly as she'd wanted to approach him—and possibly throw her arms around the poor kid and hug him—she had to be very careful with this one. One wrong move and he would completely shut her out.

From what she'd learned from his file, he was an only child who'd had the misfortune of being born to two parents who were more interested in their social status and careers than raising their son. He'd spent most of his life in boarding school or away at camp. It made a person wonder why his parents had become ensnared in a bitter custody battle. And as was usually the case, he'd landed right in the middle.

Now he was so closed off, so afraid to trust, she feared it might be too late to salvage what little self-esteem he might have had left. Four weeks wasn't nearly long enough to undo years of neglect and heartache, but she and the staff were going to give it a valiant effort.

"Mind if I join you?"

Abi looked up to find Will Bishop standing beside her table. Before she could even open her mouth to answer, he set down his plate and slid into the seat across from her. Even if she had intended to say no, he didn't give her the option. She couldn't help wondering why, of all the people in the retreat, he chose to sit with her.

Several times that day, during outdoor activities with the children, she'd had the odd sensation that someone was watching her and looked up to find him close by. He'd been engrossed in some activity and hadn't appeared to notice her, and for some baffling reason, she found herself watching him. A few times he looked up, caught her staring, and she'd quickly looked away. She had no idea what it was about him that made her feel so...*aware*. She only knew that when he was around, she couldn't seem to stop herself from looking at him, studying him.

A startling thought occurred to her. Maybe he'd sat

down at her table because he thought she was interested in him.

"Busy day?" he asked, draping his napkin in his lap.

"The first week is always a little hectic," she said, keeping her eyes glued to her plate. Why did she feel so nervous? She'd once defined her life by her ability to manipulate men. Now it unnerved her to sit three feet from one.

Maybe she was just out of practice. Although, never in her three years there had being around a male guest made her the least bit edgy.

"Are you enjoying your stay so far?" she asked, feigning great interest in the chicken on her plate.

"Is it my face?"

She was so startled by his words, her head shot up. "Your face?"

"My scars. Is that why you won't look at me?" He said it casually, as if he'd just asked her about the weather, but something dark simmered in his eyes.

"No, of course not," she said.

"It bothers some people. As if when they look directly at me, all they see are the scars." He ran one large, tanned hand down the side of his face. "I guess they don't know how to act. If they look too long, they're staring, if they look away, they're avoiding."

She surprised herself by asking, "How did it happen?"

A smile lifted the left side of his mouth. "The direct approach. That's different."

She couldn't tell if he was serious or being sarcas-

tic. It wasn't like her to be so direct—not anymore—
and it set off a siren of warning in her head. "I'm sorry.
If I'm being nosy—"

"Not at all," he said. "It was a car accident—it
caught fire. I'm lucky to be alive."

"I'm so sorry."

He shrugged. "No need to be sorry. It's not your fault."

She looked down at her plate. How did she keep
managing to say the wrong thing? The man was going
to think she was a complete flake—if he didn't already. Although maybe that would be best.

But he was a guest, so she couldn't be rude.

Will was quiet for a minute, then he said, "If my
being here makes you uncomfortable, I can move to a
different table."

"No! I'm not uncomfortable," she lied because she
didn't want to hurt his feelings. And as badly as she did
want him to get up and leave, she wanted him to stay
just as much. The warning bell clanged louder. She
didn't want to want that. It was too dangerous. She'd
done a pretty darned good job of numbing her emotions
when it came to the opposite sex. What had once been
like an addiction was now just an unpleasant memory.
If she were ever to revert back to her old ways, would
she have the strength to change back? And if she didn't,
what would become of her son?

"As long as you're sure."

"I'm sure," she said, forcing a smile.

Two chatty guests—teenage sisters from her morning session named Cindy and Leanne—joined them a
minute later, relieving them of the need to make small

talk. Yet, as hard as she tried to concentrate on her food, her eyes kept straying up to Will. She wasn't sure what it was about him that she found so fascinating. He was just so in-your-face bold. Maybe it reminded her a little bit of herself—the way she used to be. It could also be the deep hurt she saw in his eyes, a feeling she could identify with. It was second nature for her to want to heal him, to take away the pain.

Speaking of pain, she suddenly remembered Eric and looked up only to find he'd finished his dinner and was walking toward the door.

"He's a rich snob," Cindy was saying to her sister. "I don't like him."

Leanne, the younger and more reserved sister, got a dreamy look on her face. "I think he's cute."

Now this was a conversation Abi could sink her teeth into. "Who's cute?" she asked.

Leanne's cheeks turned an adorable shade of pink. She was the delicate, petite type, with long, straight brown hair she kept tucked behind her ears and she had a sweet, tranquil disposition.

"That Eric kid," Cindy said with disdain. While both girls were pretty, she was more exotic-looking, with long, shiny black hair, sparkling violet eyes and a personality to match. She also had a chip large enough to fill the Grand Canyon resting on her shoulder and, according to her file, had been getting herself into quite a bit of trouble. The normal stuff teenage girls did to get attention from their estranged parents—ditching school, experimentation with drugs and alcohol, getting involved with the wrong crowd.

Abi had already instructed the staff to keep a close eye on her. Though they were fifteen miles from the nearest town, kids like her had a knack for finding trouble where adults didn't think it existed.

"He is cute," Abi agreed and asked Leanne, "He's got that young Brad Pitt look, doesn't he?"

Leanne bit her lip and nodded, her cheeks blushing even brighter.

"He thinks he's better than everyone else," Cindy snapped.

"Why do you say that?" Abi asked.

"He won't talk to anyone! He's a total snob."

"Have you tried to talk to him?"

Cindy shrugged and said, "Why would I?"

If only she knew what Eric had been through, she might not be so quick to judge. Or maybe it wouldn't have made a difference. Either way, it would be unprofessional for Abi to divulge his private information. If he wanted to talk to them, he would in his own good time. All she could do was guide the girls and encourage them to be open-minded. Especially Cindy.

"Maybe you should try to talk to him before you go jumping to conclusions," Abi told them. "Things are not always what they seem."

"I think he's sad," Leanne said softly. "He just doesn't want anyone to know."

Cindy shook her head and rolled her eyes. "God, you are so naive."

She was definitely angry and appeared to take a lot of her frustration out on her sister. Leanne in turn only crawled deeper inside herself.

Abi glanced over at Will and saw that he was trying not to smile. In the eyes of a childless bachelor, the feminine banter must have been fairly amusing.

Abi finished her chicken, set her napkin alongside her plate and rose to her feet. "I'll see you ladies tomorrow, bright and early."

"I'll walk with you," Will said, rising to join her.

"Oh, th-that's not necessary," she said, suddenly flustered. "I'm just going to my cabin."

Will shrugged. "I don't mind. I'm in the mood for a little fresh air."

It was another sticky situation. If she said no, she could hurt his feelings. Besides, what would be the harm? It was just a casual stroll, right? Maybe he was just looking for a friendly face among strangers, and hers appealed to him somehow.

But as she nodded and they headed out of the dining room together, she had to fight back an eerie feeling of apprehension. Because she knew from experience things were not always what they seemed.

Hands tucked in his pockets, Will followed Abi out of the dining room and fell in step beside her as they walked in the direction of the employee cabins. Already the sun had begun to set and there was a nip in the air that made her shiver under her T-shirt. It would be a chilly night. A good night for sleeping.

Having been the foreman's quarters when the retreat was still a ranch, her cabin was the largest and set off by itself, tucked back several hundred feet into the woods, where enormous pines towered like sentries. It made her feel safe, and she treasured her privacy. It was the perfect home for her and Adam. She would be forever indebted to Maureen for giving them a place to stay when she'd had no place else to go, for helping her turn her life around when she'd run out of options.

"That boy they were talking about," Will said. "Eric, was it? He's had it pretty rough, huh?"

At the mere mention of his name she felt a jab to her heart. "I can't go into specifics, but yes. His life hasn't been a picnic."

"You're good with them—the kids, I mean."

"That's my job."

"No, you really care about them. That makes it more than a job."

For some reason his words made her feel all warm and soft. She did care. Sometimes too much. To the degree that it was hard to let go when their stay there ended. But it was worth it if those children walked away a little less angry or a little less hurt and confused than when they'd arrived. And there were always new kids to focus on, new activities to plan. Her son to take care of.

"What do you do for a living, Will?"

"I'm an analyst for the federal government. Homeland Security." It was about as close to the truth as Will could get without coming right out and saying he was FBI. He'd worked undercover long enough to know you stuck with the truth as often as possible. The fewer lies he had to remember, the less likely he was to make a mistake.

"Sounds exciting," she said.

"It's not. The truth is, it's a lot of paperwork and red tape."

"Where are you from?"

Small talk, he thought with a grin. He could do that. It was the first step to friendship, which was exactly what he needed from her. "I've lived in New York for the past fifteen years, but I was raised all over. I'm an Army brat." He plucked a leaf from a cluster of scrubby-looking shrubs as they walked past and slowly picked it apart. "How about you? Where do you call home?"

"I was born in New Mexico, but my mom moved us around a lot, too. This is the only real home I've had."

He wanted to ask about Maureen, but he knew it was too soon. If he pushed now, she might get suspicious. He had to gain her trust first and he was getting the feeling that might not be so simple. She walked alongside him, head lowered as if she were afraid to look him in the eye, and she kept a good two feet of mossy ground between them. Everything about her body language screamed *Back off,* so he kept his distance.

"It was hard on you?" he asked. "Moving around like that?"

"I guess. Sometimes we weren't even in one place long enough for me to make friends. Other times she'd meet someone and we'd stay a while. She married a couple of them, but it never lasted."

"My parents were married for thirty-five years when my father died—not that it was a good marriage." The words *father* and *husband* had merely been titles to Will's dad. What he'd been right up until the day he died was a glorified bully. Will had never understood why his mother had put up with it for so long. But she had, spending year after year taking orders and doing whatever she could to keep her husband happy, and he'd not been a man easily pleased.

"So many marriages aren't," she said, sounding inexplicably sad. She probably saw some pretty nasty stuff working at a place like this.

After two hellish divorces, you wouldn't catch him taking that walk down the aisle again. Wife number two had been clingy before the explosion, but in the months afterward she'd been downright unbearable. She'd cried the entire first week after the bandages had come off. She'd be fine; then she'd look at him and the tears would start to pour. He couldn't run to the store for a six-pack without her giving him the third degree, and if he wasn't back at the exact second he said he would be, she would go into hysterics.

A week before his medical leave was scheduled to end, she'd said she couldn't take it anymore and had given him an ultimatum—quit his job or pack his bags. Ironically in the span of a year it was the only time she'd ever asserted herself.

So he'd packed.

His marriage to wife number one—who he fondly referred to as "the whiner"—had ended similarly. She had always been complaining about something. He was too bossy or too unemotional or he just didn't love her enough. Then she'd gotten on her baby kick and he'd thought he'd never hear the end of it. What it boiled down to was she'd wanted babies and he hadn't been ready, and all the crying and whining and carrying on she'd done had only driven him further away. Then had come the ultimatum. *Give me a baby or pack your bags.*

So he'd packed.

His philosophy was that some people just weren't meant to be married. They weren't built that way. There was no perfect mate a person was meant to be with. It was all a crapshoot. It was luck, and he'd never been particularly lucky when it came to his personal life.

They passed a group of children coming back from the direction of the lake, and when they saw him, eyes widened and jaws hung. He was used to it. It amused him sometimes how honest children could be with their emotions. And yes, sometimes it annoyed him. Sometimes it even hurt a little.

They whispered to each other, giggled, then scurried off toward the guest cabins on the opposite end of the resort.

"I think I'm going to have a talk with those kids about manners," Abi said, her tone so sharp and biting it surprised him. "That kind of behavior is unacceptable."

Will brushed it off with a wave of his hand. "It happens all the time. It's normal for kids to be afraid or curious about things or people that look different. It's human nature."

For the first time since they'd begun walking she looked up at him. "There's nothing they can do? About the scars, I mean."

"They considered doing a skin graft, but they

couldn't guarantee how good it would look. There was talk about infection and complications. I could lose sight in that eye and end up with even more nerve damage. I decided I would rather leave it this way than take my chances. I figure it gives my face character."

She smiled up at him—a genuine and open smile. Even in the fading light he could see that her eyes were really quite remarkable. What he'd believed was a dull brown upon closer inspection was really a spectrum of browns and greens and yellows.

"That's a nice way to look at it. Not many people are that comfortable in their own skin." She gestured past the other cabins, into the woods. "I live over there."

They turned down a narrow path that led to the large cabin nestled back among the trees. The front porch spanned the entire width of the house, and a wood swing hung from its eaves. The temperature dropped as they walked deeper under the trees, and the scent of pine and moss filled the air. He found himself slowing his steps, prolonging their inevitable parting. She was a little closer now. If he were to sway slightly to the right, he might bump arms with her. For some reason the idea of touching her held an almost irresistible appeal.

"This is home," she said.

"Cozy." Despite growing up in urban areas, it had always been a dream of his to live somewhere like this. Somewhere serene and peaceful, away from the hectic pace of the city.

Someday, when he retired maybe.

"The first time I saw this place I fell in love with it,"

she said, her face the picture of tranquility, until she glanced up at him and the shutters came down again.

"My face really does bother you, doesn't it?"

"No, I just…" She bit her lip and lowered her eyes to the ground. "I don't know what my problem is."

"You know," he said as they reached the porch, "when a child is frightened by my face, when they don't know how to act, I have a trick to put them at ease."

"You do?"

"Give me your hand," he said, and she gave him a wary look. "It won't hurt, I promise."

Reluctantly she held it out. Her fingers were long and graceful-looking, her nails short, clean and neat. He took her hand between both of his, and she tensed.

"I don't bite." Lifting her hand to his face, he flattened her palm against his cheek. First her eyes went wide, then she blinked with surprise. He circled her wrist so she wouldn't pull away. "It's okay," he said. "Touch it."

Very gently, as if she thought it might sting, she brushed her fingers over the side of his face.

"See, it's just skin."

"It doesn't hurt?"

"I had some nerve damage, so I really don't feel much of anything. Extreme hot and cold mostly. And pressure." He gave her the crooked grin that had become his trademark since the accident. "The left side of my mouth doesn't always cooperate, either. But I have less area to shave, so it does have its positive points."

She gave him a shy grin. "The skin, it's almost... soft."

He let his hand slip from her wrist, expecting her to pull away, but she didn't. Instead she lifted her hand higher, ran her thumb over the deep scar that split his eyebrow in half.

A tiny wrinkle formed between her brows. "So close to your eye."

"Yeah, it's a miracle I didn't lose it." He watched her as she gently explored his face. Her skin was tan, and the beginnings of crow's-feet marked the corners of her eyes, meaning she was probably older than he'd originally thought. Her cheekbones were high, her mouth wide. With a little color for emphasis, her lips could even be described as lush—especially when she smiled. She was neither tall nor short. Neither heavy nor thin.

Individually her features were ordinary, but all put together, there was something about her, something almost...*sexy*. Which was weird because at first glance she'd seemed one of the least sexy woman he'd ever met.

Her eyes locked on his and her lips parted slightly, and something in the air shifted. He couldn't even be sure what it was that had changed, all he knew was that he wanted to touch her. He wanted to smooth his fingers over her face, brush his thumb over the softness of her lower lip.

He wanted to kiss her.

Her eyes darkened a shade and her lids slipped down, as if they were too heavy to hold open, and her gaze strayed to his mouth. He found himself wondering what she would taste like, if it would be slow and sweet or hot and wild.

Definitely slow and sweet, he decided. She wasn't the hot-and-wild type at all.

Unconsciously he lowered his head, and she must have read his thoughts because the spell was instantly broken. The guard she wore snapped back down over her eyes, and she pulled her hand away from his face.

"I—I have to go." She backed up the porch steps. In the fading light he could see her eyes were like saucers, as if he'd scared the holy hell out of her.

Let her go, his conscience warned him. He'd pushed too far too fast. On the bright side, at least she was looking at him now. Looking at him as though he was the devil incarnate.

A little bit of damage control might even be in order.

"I'm sorry if I made you uncomfortable," he told her.

"I'm not uncomfortable," she said.

She was lying, but he let it go. He thought about shaking her hand, but everything in her stance said to back off.

He tucked his hands back into his pockets instead. "Thanks for keeping me company. I'm sure I'll see you around."

"See you."

He turned and started down the path toward the main building, but he couldn't help shooting once last glance over his shoulder.

She was already gone.

* * *

Abi closed the door and fell against it, holding a trembling hand over her wildly beating heart. Will had been about to kiss her. He'd even dipped his head a little.

She should recognize the signs; she'd seen the move a million times. Though she didn't remember the thought of a kiss ever making her this weak in the knees before, the idea of intimacy with a man sparking this feeling of giddy anticipation. Not even her first time in the bed of Bo Reily's pickup truck—of course, he'd had her so liquored up on Jack Daniel's she hadn't felt much of anything then.

She'd had enough sex in her life for five women, but she'd never touched a man the way she had Will, never felt the kind of intimacy she had with her hand on his face. Sex had been nothing but a vehicle to get what she wanted, a way to bend men to her will.

You use what assets God gave you, her mother used to tell her, and Tara Sullivan would know. She'd spent her life hopping from one man's bed to another, and Abi had learned the apple never fell far from the tree.

She hadn't known she could *feel* this way. This hot, excited, restless feeling that seemed to come from somewhere deep in her bones.

She'd felt something else, too. She'd felt vulnerable, and that scared her half to death.

She'd gone four years without a man in her bed, four years spent reprogramming her brain to reject the idea of sex in any form. And in the span of five minutes Will had undone it all. The woman she used to be, the one she'd thought was long dead and buried, was still sneaking around inside her somewhere.

God help her if she ever found a way out.

But she didn't need a man to take care of her anymore. She'd proven to herself through determination and hard work that she was a survivor, and no one could take that away from her.

Brittney, Adam's babysitter, appeared in his bedroom doorway and came down the hall toward her. "I thought I heard you come in. He had his bath and he's playing in his room if you want to—" She stopped short. "Holy cow, Abi, you look like you've seen a ghost."

A ghost. Huh. She couldn't have put it better herself. "You know, Brit, I think I just did."

Chapter 3

Abi breathed in the clean afternoon air, feeling the burn in her calves as she hiked with a group of a dozen kids—the ten-years-and-older group—along the nature trail at the foothills of the mountain and into the woods. All around her the forest was alive with sights and sounds and scents. Four years ago she never would have appreciated the simple beauty of it. She would have seen it as dirty and smelly and uncivilized.

Now it was her solace.

It still amazed her at times, the changes she'd made in her life. It hadn't been easy, and she never wanted to go back to being that lost, confused young woman she had once been. At the time she'd thought she owned the world, but it had all been an illusion.

"Go talk to him," she heard Leanne whisper.

"I told you, he's a snob." Cindy gave her younger sister a shove. "If you like him so much, you go talk to him."

Abi watched the exchange from the back of the group where she walked with the younger kids. It was easy to see that the older sister was the dominant, outgoing sibling, and like Abi at sixteen, she probably considered herself an authority on the workings of the teenage male mind. As pretty as she was, Abi didn't doubt Cindy had her fair share of attention from the opposite sex. What need would she have to go looking for it?

Despite her confidence and nonchalant demeanor, she was probably the one hurt the most deeply by their parents' divorce. She was just better at hiding it. At least, that was usually the case. Leanne, on the other hand, wore her emotions right out in the open for everyone to see.

Though it was Cindy who Abi could identify with, it was Leanne who intrigued her. And she hoped the younger girl would work up the courage to talk to Eric. Since arriving he still hadn't talked to anyone. Abi was biding her time, waiting for just the right moment to approach him.

She glanced over her shoulder and saw that he was still there, lagging behind, eyes firmly fixed on the ground. She worried about him staying in a cabin all by himself. Not that she thought he couldn't take care of himself. He wasn't known to be a troublemaker and at seventeen he was old enough to stay there alone.

That was exactly what worried her. The isolation.

She had the feeling he led a very lonely existence to begin with. Would this only make things worse?

She felt a tug on her shirt and turned to find the youngest boy in the group, a ten-year-old named Noah, walking beside her.

"Miss Abi, I'm tired and my feet hurt. I want to go back."

Though he was a sweet kid, he was quickly gaining a reputation as a whiner.

She rumpled the back of his blond head and gave him an encouraging smile. "We'll be taking a break real soon. Can you hold out another couple of minutes?"

"Okay," Noah sighed, then, shoulders slumped, he ambled off. From what Abi had heard, Noah's father had replaced his wife and son with his much younger, pregnant mistress, and Noah's mother was so beside herself with grief and resentment she could barely function. Noah had lost not only his father but the attention of his mother, as well. Financially they were set, but as Abi had learned, money didn't buy happiness. It didn't heal wounded hearts or erase past mistakes. In fact, it had a way of causing more trouble than it was worth.

Hopefully with therapy and time to heal Noah's mother would come to realize how much her son needed her, and they would leave the retreat a little less heartbroken. It was the best Abi could hope for.

"Have you got room for one more?"

Startled by the familiar voice, Abi looked back to find Will Bishop walking briskly up the trail behind them. He wore green cargo shorts and a dark tank that showed off the lean muscles in his shoulders and arms. Her heart gave a funny little flutter at the sight of him.

What was he doing here? Granted, the trail was a frequently traveled one, but she couldn't help wondering if he'd followed them.

The idea both excited and concerned her.

She was still embarrassed by her behavior when he'd walked her to her cabin last night and had decided it would be best to keep her distance for the remainder of his stay. She'd had a speech rehearsed at lunch to let him down gently, but he had barely spoken to her. Just a friendly hello as he'd walked past her to a different table. Later, every time she'd looked at him—which she found herself doing more often than she was comfortable with—he had been engaged in conversation with another guest or staff member and hadn't seemed to know she existed. Maybe she'd imagined the whole thing and he really hadn't been thinking about kissing her. She used to be able to spot that kind of thing a mile away, but perhaps her feminine radar was rustier than she'd thought.

So odds were he hadn't followed her but was instead out for a stroll and just happened to run into them. Which was good. She'd never had a guest interested in her, though it was known to happen, and the idea made her uncomfortable. The fact that she found him so fascinating was even worse.

"We're taking a nature hike," she said as he walked up and fell in step beside her. He was tall and fit and the way he moved was almost hypnotizing. She would have gone as far as to say he was graceful had he not been so glaringly masculine. She'd never known a man who displayed so much confidence with such a complete lack of arrogance.

"Shouldn't you be in group therapy?"

Will shrugged and made a face. "Therapy isn't really my thing."

Interesting attitude considering he was at a retreat that specialized in therapeutic counseling. "Maybe it's none of my business, but if you don't want therapy, what are you doing here?"

He thought about that for a minute. "I'm not sure, really. I just knew I needed some time to work things through, to make some changes in my life. This seemed like the right place to do it—where I'm with people who understand what I'm going through."

Well, she gave him points for honesty. "You should really consider it," she said. "The therapy, I mean. It's probably not what you would expect."

"I'll think about it," he said.

They reached the clearing where her group would take their first rest. Overturned logs and tree stumps served as seats. "Okay, everyone, fifteen-minute break. I'd like you to take out your journals and write at least one page."

"What do we have to write about?" one of the younger girls asked.

"Anything you'd like. It could be a page about something you saw in the woods that interested you or something you're feeling. Anything at all." It didn't really matter what they wrote. Their journals were a warm-up exercise to get the kids loosened up and ready for their group therapy sessions later that afternoon.

The kids dropped their backpacks to fish out their journals, and Abi turned to Will. "You don't have to wait."

"I don't mind." He set his pack on the ground and sat on an overturned log.

Okay.

Whether she wanted his company or not, it didn't look as if she had much choice now, not without causing a scene and possibly insulting or embarrassing him in front of the kids. Besides, what could be the harm in a little friendly conversation?

"Keeps to himself, doesn't he?" Will asked.

She followed the direction of his gaze and saw Eric standing alone, leaning against a tree away from the group. He hadn't taken out his journal and was instead whacking at the underbrush with a stick, his usual bored expression on his face.

Rather than insist, she let him be. Forcing him would only make matters worse.

She sat beside Will on the log. "I haven't figured out how to approach him yet. I know there's a way in, I just have to find it."

Will leaned back and stretched his legs out in front of him. They were long and muscular and covered with crisp dark hair. She'd never been particularly attracted to men's legs before, but she found her eyes drawn to his and even had a difficult time looking away. What was it about him that fascinated her so?

"He's a problem kid?" Will asked.

Though she tried not to discuss one guest with another, she was grateful for the neutral topic. And being male, Will might have an idea how she could get through to a teenage boy. "The opposite, in fact. His parents are concerned because he's become unusually introverted. They sent him here to pull him out of his shell."

"Sent him here? I thought it was supposed to be family therapy."

"It is usually."

"Let me guess—the parents don't have time."

"Something like that."

He shook his head. "That's too bad."

"Miss Abi!" Noah appeared in front of them, hopping from one foot to the other, clutching the front of his shorts. "I gotta pee bad."

Add drama queen to his personality quirks. All he had to do was ask.

"That's the cool thing about being a boy. Outdoor plumbing." She nodded toward the dense forest on either side of the clearing. "You've got a couple hundred trees to choose from."

He glanced around, a worried look on his face. "I don't want to go out there alone."

"Would you like me to come with you?"

His expression went from worried to horrified. "Yuck! You're a girl."

"Would you like Mr. Bishop to take you?"

He looked Will over in the blatant, honest way that kids did, then shook his head. "He's a stranger."

"Hmm," she looked around, wondering how to solve this problem, then got an idea. "What if one of the older boys took you? Would that be okay?"

Noah considered that for a minute, then nodded.

"How about Eric?

"Yeah, okay."

Perfect. Just the way in she needed. "Eric," she called, "can I see you for a minute?"

His expression one of sheer disinterest, Eric tossed down his stick, shoved both hands in the pockets of his shorts and ambled over to them. Though he was only seventeen, he stood close to six feet tall. His sun-streaked brown hair was on the long side, and he brushed it aside with a jerk of his head when it fell into his eyes. "Yeah?"

He was trying so hard to not look lost and lonely, it broke her heart.

"Noah here needs to relieve himself, but he's uncomfortable with the idea of a girl or a stranger taking him," she explained. "Could you please take him far enough into the woods so he has some privacy?"

He shrugged as if it didn't matter either way to him. "Sure. Come on, kid."

He headed into the woods and Noah trailed behind him. Abi could hear him jabbering away. Maybe he would get Eric talking.

"That was good," Will said.

Abi turned back to him and smiled. "Like I said, the moment would present itself. I just had to be patient."

"You're really good with the kids."

"I love my job. Although, if you had told me four years ago that I would be doing this, I'd have said you were nuts."

"Why is that?"

"Let's just say I wasn't into kids back then."

"A lot of things can change in four years," he agreed, a sad, almost wistful look in his eyes.

"Is that when it happened?"

He turned to her. "What happened?"

"The car accident."

"Yeah, four years ago." Four years next month, in fact. The anniversary of Ryan's death. In an odd way it felt as if Will's life had been on hold since then, as though he were just biding his time, waiting until Vince was brought to justice. He was so close now he could feel the heavy hand of justice by his side, waiting for him to succeed. And he would get that justice, no matter the consequences.

"How did you end up working here?" he asked her.

"Fate." She looked over at him, and though she smiled, he could see the guarded look in her eyes. She was hiding something, and he had a pretty good idea it had to do with her boss.

After talking with many of the other staff members, he'd concluded that not many seemed to know much about their elusive employer, and the few who did weren't inclined to discuss her.

He was all the more convinced that Abi was the key, his ticket to meeting Maureen. But it wasn't going to be a simple operation. There was something about her, something in her eyes he identified with—a connection he felt—and he was pretty certain the feeling was mutual. But he was also aware that his presence made her uneasy, as if she wasn't quite sure what to make of him. That was okay, because he wasn't sure what to make of her either—what he found so attractive about a woman so plain and unassuming. His wives might have been clingy and dependant, but they were both physically beautiful.

Today Abi wore her hair in a ponytail, her face once again scrubbed clean—he'd never once seen her wear makeup. Her clothes were on the baggy side, as if she were self-conscious about her body and deliberately tried to hide her figure. As far as he could see, she wasn't overweight. In fact, she was so slight in stature, he was surprised by the muscle tone in her legs. He was guessing that she'd done a fair amount of hiking to develop calves like that.

Working undercover he'd learned to subtly—and sometimes not so subtly—insinuate himself into any given situation. He knew just how far to push and when to back off. He didn't doubt he would get what he wanted. He'd waited too long, worked too hard to let this chance slip away. And there was no rush. He had the better part of four weeks to get what he needed. Plenty of time to win Abi's trust.

"I guess I should be on my way." He stood and hiked his backpack up over his shoulders. "I'd like to get a few miles in before I play golf."

He looked down at Abi and for a second he could swear he saw disappointment in her eyes.

"There's a sign-up sheet in the office for both individual and group therapy," she told him. "I'd like you to consider it."

"I will," he said, knowing he really wouldn't. He didn't need a shrink to tell him he wasn't cut out for marriage. He'd figured that out all by himself. "Maybe I'll see you at dinner tonight."

She gave him a noncommittal smile that said whether he did or didn't was of no consequence to her. "See you around."

That he would definitely do. She could count on it.

Chapter 4

"Ms. Sullivan?"

Abi looked up from the file on her cluttered desk to the young man standing in her office doorway. The red T-shirt he had draped over his shoulder bore the retreat logo, meaning he was probably her new employee. According to his employee file he was barely twenty, and she didn't make a habit out of ogling men ten years her junior, yet she couldn't help feeling a tad breathless by the sight of him. Jet-black hair with dark, deepset eyes to match. Tall and muscular in all the right places. A real heartbreaker. "You must be Tom."

"Tom Sterling." He dropped his duffel bag and walked toward her, hand outstretched, flashing her a lazy, brilliant white smile.

Oh, yeah, this guy was going to drive the female

counselors into a tizzy. But considering his shining recommendations, he would be worth the hassle.

Abi stood and took his hand. His grip was firm and confident. "Welcome to Healing Hearts. I appreciate you coming on such short notice."

"It's me who should be thanking you. My scholarship doesn't cover living expenses, so when my last position fell through, I was kind of desperate."

"I was just looking over your file. Your references are impeccable. As I explained on the phone, you'll be working primarily with the younger kids."

"Okay," he said.

"Great." She pulled open the file drawer and took out a copy of the employee handbook. "This will cover what we didn't discuss on the phone. If you have any questions, you can ask me or any of the other staff." In fact, she was sure the female employees would be falling all over themselves to accommodate him.

"Go see Susie in the main office. She'll see that you get settled in. I'll give you the rest of the day to acquaint yourself to the grounds. You report for work eight o'clock tomorrow morning in the children's activities center."

He took the handbook. "Thanks, Ms. Sullivan."

"Just Abi," she said. "I'll see you bright and early."

He shot her one more heart-stopping, slightly shy grin, then grabbed his bag and headed out the door.

Abi picked up the phone and dialed Susie's extension. "Susie, I sent Tom your way. Could you have one of the counselors show him to his cabin and get him settled in?"

"Sure thing, Abi. What do you think of him? Is he cute or what?"

"He's going to wreak havoc on the female staff."

"If I were ten years younger…" she said with a wistful sigh before she hung up.

Abi knew exactly what she meant. Seeing a young man like Tom, with his entire future ahead of him—it made her feel so…old. As if the best years of her life had been wasted. If she could only go back, knowing then what she knew now. She would have done things so differently.

But there was no point dwelling on the past. Some things you just couldn't change.

Abi checked the sign-up sheets in the office and shook her head. "Darn it."

Susie looked up from her computer monitor. "Something wrong?"

"I don't suppose Will Bishop has been in here today."

"The guy with the face? Nope, haven't seen him. Why do you ask?"

"I was just hoping he signed up for therapy, but I don't see his name here."

"Maybe he just hasn't gotten around to it yet."

"Yeah, maybe." She'd seen him heading toward the golf course with a group of men that afternoon and later she'd seen him walking toward the lake, a towel draped over his shoulder. She'd really hoped he would find time to stop in the office, but at least he seemed to be making friends. Maybe one of the other men would persuade him to join a group. She had the feeling that deep down he knew he needed therapy. Why else would he be here? All he needed was a nudge to get the ball rolling.

"Where's Adam?" Susie asked.

"He's with the tot group down by the beach. They're having a picnic dinner. There's a little boy who's four, so Adam has a new best friend. He just loves it when the new family sessions start. Would you do me a favor and let me know if Will signs up?"

"Sure thing, Abi."

Abi left the office and headed for the main dining room. It was the first Tuesday of the session, meaning it was Italian cuisine night. Though meals were served buffet-style, the food was delicious. Despite that Abi had a full kitchen in her cabin, it was usually easier to eat in the dining room with the guests and other staff. However, she tried at least two or three times a week to have a special dinner for just her and Adam—a family night when they would eat together, then sit on the family room floor and play board games or cards or do crafts. Then he would climb into bed and she would read him books until he fell asleep.

Sometimes she would sit and watch him sleep, memorizing every detail of his precious face. Though being a single parent could be rough, she couldn't imagine her life without him in it.

Abi fixed herself a plate with linguine in clam sauce and a slice of toasted garlic bread, then went to find a table, scanning the room, telling herself she wasn't looking for Will—and denying a dash of disappointment when she didn't see him there. He'd mentioned seeing her at dinner, although that didn't mean he'd planned to sit with her. In fact, she didn't want him to sit with her.

Well, maybe she did a little, but she knew it would be best if he didn't. He had stirred in her feelings she'd locked away a long time ago. What scared her even more—he made her feel things she'd *never* felt before.

She headed for an empty table near the back, set her plate down and took a seat.

Even if he had been there and she had wanted to sit with him, she probably wouldn't have had the guts to approach his table and sit down. The old Abi, the one she'd been before she'd had Adam, would have strutted into the room, happy only when she knew all eyes were turned her way. She wouldn't have hesitated inviting herself to sit with any man she chose. Of course, she never would have chosen a man like Will. She'd been attracted to men with money and power. Men who served a purpose.

In the end, all it had gotten her was trouble, and she realized now she was better off alone. No man was worth what she had been through.

If that was true, why did she find her eyes straying toward the door? Why did her heart flutter with nerves when she thought about seeing Will step into the room? When she remembered the way he looked at her? She couldn't help wondering what it was he saw. Her days of a flat stomach and twenty-four-inch waist had left her for good in the fourth month of her pregnancy, when the morning sickness had ended and her appetite had returned with a vengeance.

Rather than feel disgusted by her expanding figure, she'd felt free. She'd said goodbye to the daily torture of exercising herself to death, to the diet of lettuce and water. With every pound she'd gained, every stretch mark that had appeared on her flawless skin, she'd felt more content, more in control of her life. She was more comfortable in her skin now than she'd ever been.

Maybe some men—men like Will—found that attractive.

Or maybe she was delusional.

Forcing herself to concentrate on her plate and not the door, she shoveled a bite of creamy pasta into her mouth. She would hurry up and eat, go pick up Adam, then call it an early night. It sounded like a pretty good plan, until her eyes strayed up once again and landed right on Will coming through the dining room door. As much as she wanted to look away, she felt frozen in place.

He stopped just inside the doorway and gazed around the room. *He's not looking for me,* she told herself, *just a vacant place to sit.* Then his eyes stopped on her and held there, a grin quirking up one corner of his mouth. Her stomach did a hard flop and the hair on the back of her neck shivered to attention. There was a boyish charm to his smile, but there was no doubt in her mind he was all man.

He held her gaze for a few seconds more, then headed for the buffet to fix himself a plate. She forced herself to keep her head down, eyes on her food. Just because he'd looked *at* her, it didn't mean he'd been looking *for* her. It didn't mean he wanted to sit with her, and she didn't want to encourage him by making eye contact again. He'd already caught her staring at him far too many times.

She took another bite of pasta but had trouble swallowing past the knot of anxiety that had lodged itself in her throat—an almost giddy, nervous, excited feeling that didn't want to go away.

"Is this seat taken?"

Abi looked up to find Will standing beside the table, gesturing to the seat beside her, and her heart began to beat double time. So he did want to sit with her. But was it a good idea? She didn't want to be rude. It wasn't his fault she had some sort of weird fascination with him.

"Um, no," she said, inviting him to sit.

He pulled out the chair and sat down, so casual and at ease, she felt silly for feeling nervous. His hair was damp and he smelled like some sort of masculine soap. "How did the rest of the hike go this afternoon?"

"It was good." she said, trying to look not at him but at her food.

"Looks like Eric has a new friend."

Abi followed the direction of Will's gaze and saw Eric sitting across the room with Noah. Noah was gabbing away about something, his mouth moving a mile a minute. He'd been stuck to Eric's side the second half of the hike and had followed him around like a lost puppy the rest of the afternoon. It had to be driving Eric crazy by now, but he sat quietly listening to Noah yammer on.

As she'd suspected, he was a good kid at heart.

"I was just in the office," she told Will. "I didn't see your name on the sign-up sheet."

He flashed that crooked grin. "Checking up on me, huh?"

She refused to be rattled by his charm. "That's my job."

"I said I would think about it."

"And?"

He shrugged. "And I'm still thinking."

"Mommy!"

Abi looked up to find Adam barreling toward her, his little legs carrying him as quickly as they could, followed by Renee, one of the junior counselors. As it always did, her heart filled with so much love and pride at the sight of his happy face she thought it might burst. She'd never truly learned to love until she'd become a mother. Until she'd felt her baby kick the first time. Until he was born and she'd gazed down into his perfect little face, counted all ten fingers and toes. It was then that she'd finally felt complete, as if she'd found her purpose.

He was the only thing in the world that mattered to her now.

Adam launched himself into her arms and she pulled him up in her lap, ruffling his short dark hair. "Hey, kiddo, did you have a good picnic?"

"I made you a present!" Adam said, squirming excitedly. "Show her, Renee!"

"Okay, okay," Renee said with a laugh, handing Abi Adam's latest creation—several Popsicle sticks glued together to form an abstract shape covered with blue and gold glitter. Some of it flaked off and landed on her plate.

Renee cringed. "Sorry about that. He couldn't wait to show you."

"It's okay," Abi told her.

"Do you like it, Mommy?"

"I love it, honey." She gave Adam a big squeeze. "Thank you."

"Would you like me to take him back to the activity center while you finish your dinner?" Renee asked her.

"That's okay. I'm almost finished."

"Okay. See you tomorrow, Adam." She turned and headed for the door.

"Who are you?" Adam asked, and Abi realized he was talking to Will. If the look of surprise on Will's face was any indication, he'd had no idea she had a child. Abi had found if there was one sure way to detract a man's interest, it was to introduce him to her son. They couldn't get away fast enough.

In a small way she was disappointed—but relieved, too.

"Adam, this is Mr. Bishop. He's a guest here. Will, this is Adam, my son."

Will recovered from his surprise and flashed Adam a smile that for the most part looked genuine, then stuck out a hand for him to shake. "Nice to meet you, Adam."

Adam shook his hand, then cocked his head, giving Will a scrutinizing look. "Your face looks funny."

Abi cringed. "Adam, that's not polite."

"It's okay," Will told her. "He's right. It does look funny."

"You look like a villain," Adam said.

Will laughed. "A villain?"

"He looks like a bad guy. You know, like in a comic book." He narrowed his eyes at Will. "You're not a villain, are you?"

Will laughed. "No, I'm definitely one of the good guys."

Satisfied with that, Adam turned to Abi. "Can I have a cookie?"

"Just one," she told him, giving his behind a playful swat as he hopped off her lap and darted for the buffet table. She turned to Will. "Sorry about that. Three-year-olds can be brutally honest."

"That's okay. I didn't know you had a son."

"You didn't ask."

The corner of his mouth quirked up. "You're right, I didn't."

"If you want to leave, I won't be offended."

He looked puzzled. "Leave?"

"If you'd like to sit at another table."

"Why would I do that?"

"It's a natural reaction when men find out I have a son. They're gone so fast they leave skid marks."

"I think you'll find I'm not like most men."

She was getting that idea already. He was unlike any man she'd ever known. She couldn't decide if that was a good or a bad thing.

"The truth is, I like you, Abi. Your having a child doesn't change that."

And there lies the problem, she thought. Because she liked him, too. They would both be better off if he'd seen her son and made a run for it.

She gazed around nervously, hoping no one was hearing their conversation. No one seemed to be paying any attention to them. "Will, I don't think this is a good idea."

He took a bite of his pasta and wiped his mouth with his napkin. "You don't think what is a good idea?"

"This. Us. It's against retreat policy for a staff member to become…involved with a guest."

"Involved?"

"I think you know what I mean."

He flashed a grin that bordered on bashful. "Yes, Abi, I'm attracted to you, but I'm not here looking for a relationship. It's the last thing on my mind."

She couldn't help feeling a little warm and fuzzy knowing Will found her attractive. She'd suspected, but to hear him come right out and say it validated her somehow. It had been a long time since any man had regarded her in a sexual way.

Despite her efforts to look as unappealing as possible to the opposite sex, Will saw something in her, something deeper than physical beauty. Something she hadn't even known was there—and probably hadn't been four years ago. She'd changed so much since then.

The fact that he was as wary of his feelings toward her as she was about her feelings toward him made her less uncomfortable. "I appreciate your honesty," she told him.

"What about friendship? Is that against the rules, too?"

She'd never really thought about it. She'd formed very tight bonds with some of the kids and a few superficial relationships with adult guests in the past—mostly the women. It wasn't something she avoided or encouraged. Maybe that wouldn't be so bad.

The only problem was, nothing about her encounters with Will felt superficial.

"I've always considered myself a likable guy, but if you don't want to be friends with me, if I've offended you somehow—"

"No, it's not that. I just…" She clasped her hands on the table. "I've just had some bad experiences with men in the past. I guess you could say that I'm jaded."

Will laid his hand over both of hers, and a jolt of sensation shot up her arms. She had to fight not to yank them away. How could such a simple touch make her feel so deeply aware? Aware of the blood pulsing through her veins as her heartbeat quickened, aware of the slow rise of heat from her breasts, up her throat and into her face. Aware that no man had ever touched her so innocently yet so deeply.

"The truth is," he said, "I've had some pretty lousy experiences with women in the past. Maybe it could be therapeutic for both of us."

To imagine that he was as vulnerable as she was eased her concerns, if only a little. And he made a good point. Maybe this wouldn't be such a bad thing. It had been so long since she'd trusted a man. Maybe a friendship with Will would be good for her. Maybe she could put the last of her ghosts to rest and feel like a whole person again. And maybe it would be good for Adam to get to know him. To teach him that despite having a disfigurement, Will was like everyone else.

On the surface anyway. To her, he was unlike any man she'd ever known.

"What do you say?" Will asked. "Friends?"

His smile was so charming, his friendliness so contagious and the hopeful look in his eyes so endearing, she could hardly tell him no.

"Yes," she agreed. "I guess we could be friends."

Will smiled, feeling only slightly guilty. But he hadn't lied to her, hadn't misled her in any way. He *did* want to be her friend. He just hadn't been forthcoming about his reasons.

She'd been right about one thing. In a normal situation if he discovered a woman he'd taken out had a kid, her number landed in the nearest trash can. Not that he didn't like kids. After Ryan died, he'd tried to spend as much time as he could with his kids, to fill the void of losing their father at least a little. They'd grown to consider him an uncle, until their mother had remarried last year and he'd felt uncomfortable coming around. Her new husband was a good guy and needed a chance to bond with the kids, so Will had made himself scarce. It had surprised him how much he'd missed them.

But since he had no plans to take another trip down the aisle, he liked to keep his relationships with women as uncomplicated as possible. That was tough when there were kids involved. If they got attached, it was one more person to hurt after the relationship had run its course.

Unfortunately this time it was unavoidable. Not that he was planning on getting involved with Abi on anything but a friendly level. He didn't have time for emotional entanglements, not with so much at stake. Besides, with the exception of amiable working relationships with a few female agents, he'd never been simply friends with a woman. Not that he'd intentionally avoided friendships with women. Maybe it was a side effect of being raised by a man who'd viewed women as second-class citizens.

Will's father, an Army drill sergeant, had had no respect for Will's mom—or any woman, for that matter. He had run the household like an army barrack. And though he'd never laid a hand on her—he'd saved that for his son—his words had done more damage than any fist in the gut. His put-downs and insults had connected harder, stung deeper than any slap across the face.

And though Will was ashamed to admit it, as hard as he'd tried to be different from his old man, he'd carried a few of his old habits into his own marriages. He had no patience for the whims of the opposite sex.

He didn't doubt that if he'd made a lousy husband, he'd make an even worse father. Even if he didn't mean to.

"Well, I should get Adam home." Abi stood and dropped her napkin on the table. "I guess I'll see you around."

He noticed she'd barely touched her food. Not that it looked all that appetizing with a glitter garnish.

He had half a notion to offer to walk her back to her cabin and then maybe invite himself in for an after-dinner drink, but he didn't want to push his luck and make her suspicious. He had to take this slowly.

He looked up at her and smiled. "I'll see you tomorrow?"

"Probably."

He watched her cross the room and collect her son, stopping briefly to chat with a few guests. Then she shot him a glance and a vague smile before she disappeared through the dining room door. She sometimes looked so wary, like a frightened mouse. Other times she was startlingly direct.

It puzzled him.

He had the feeling there was more to this woman than met the eye. And as with any good mystery, he felt the insatiable need to solve it.

Chapter 5

"Eric, could you give me a hand over here?" Abi called from the woodpile by the maintenance building.

Eric ambled over from where he stood alone watching the other kids play volleyball. Since that first time he'd helped her out with Noah two days ago, she'd been asking small favors here and there, and gradually Eric was beginning to open up to her. Just a few casual words, but it was a start. She only wished he would open up to the other kids, realize that they had the same feelings he did and that it was okay to talk about it. That it would probably make being here so much easier.

"What do you need?" he asked.

"I need a couple of cartsful of wood hauled down to the beach for the bonfire Friday night. Would you mind helping me?"

He shrugged, which she took as his way of saying yes, and together they started piling wood into the cart.

Movement a few feet away caught her attention, and she looked up to see Leanne casually stroll past. A warm, gentle summer breeze tousled her shoulder-length brown hair as she gazed at the sky, the trees, the lake shimmering in the afternoon sun. Everywhere but the one place Abi knew she was aching to look—at Eric.

Where you found Eric, Leanne wasn't far away looking lovesick and wistful.

Leanne stopped and crouched down to tie a tennis-shoe lace that Abi was pretty sure hadn't come loose. The poor kid was just begging to be noticed.

As far as Abi could tell, Leanne hadn't yet worked up the courage to speak to Eric. Abi could only hope that if and when Leanne did, Eric would be receptive to her.

She turned to him and nearly dropped a log on her foot when she realized he was watching Leanne.

Interesting.

Maybe all they needed was a little push, someone to get the ball rolling. But how? What could she do so the whole thing didn't feel like a setup? She gazed around, searching for a reason to leave the two of them alone, and found it. He was walking toward her from the direction of the main building, his hands tucked casually into his shorts pockets, looking tanned and healthy and—heaven help her—good enough to eat.

And his timing couldn't have been better.

"Will," she said, giving him a bright smile. "You

must be here to discuss that thing we talked about the other day."

His brow wrinkled with confusion. "Thing?"

"You know, that thing we were discussing during dinner." She widened her eyes, hoping he would get the message. "I could spare a few minutes right now if you have time."

"Oh, that. Right." He still looked confused but played along. "Yeah, now would be great."

She turned to Eric. "I'm sorry to dump this on you. I just need to talk to Mr. Bishop for a few minutes."

Eric gave her his "whatever" shrug and kept tossing logs onto the cart.

She looked over at Leanne, who was still crouched a few yards away and appeared to have found something of great interest in the grass. "Leanne, could you come over here?"

Leanne jerked to her feet and turned to Abi. When she saw Eric looking at her, her eyes instantly lowered to the ground. She walked over to where they stood. "Yeah, Abi?"

"Could you help Eric load the cart with wood and take it down to the fire pit?"

"Okay," Leanne said softly, eyes still downcast, her face ten different shades of red.

"Two loads should cover it," Abi said, figuring that would give them time to get acquainted, then decided, what the heck? "On second thought, why don't you make that four? And don't forget about group therapy at three sharp."

She walked away from the maintenance building,

Will at her side. When they were out of hearing range he said, "I take it you don't really have something to discuss with me."

"Nope."

"You're not matchmaking, are you?"

"Matchmaking is such a misleading word," she said. "I was…"

"Meddling?"

She shot him an exasperated look. "*No.* Neither is taking the initiative to meet the other."

He nodded. "I see. So you're doing it for them?"

"Kind of."

He looked down at her and grinned. "Like I said, you're meddling."

She smiled back. "Yeah, okay, maybe a little."

"In that case, I guess we should at least try to look like we have something to discuss." They walked slowly alongside each other.

"So what's the deal with those two?" he asked, nodding toward Eric and Leanne.

"He's so withdrawn and she's so shy. I thought they might understand each other. Sometimes if a kid has a friend to talk to, he or she is more likely to open up during group therapy."

"You really push the therapy, don't you?"

"Of course. It's an integral part of the retreat."

"Retreat…therapy." He shook his head. "I don't know, the two just don't seem synonymous. When I think of a retreat, I think of relaxing—a vacation. How relaxed can you be when someone is shrinking your head?"

"You shouldn't knock something until you try it," she said.

He slipped his hands into the pockets of his shorts and his elbow brushed against her arm. It was a completely innocent move, but it made her realize just how close they were walking and she casually moved away. What would the staff think if they saw her so cozy with a guest? Not that bumping elbows was considered cozy. Maybe she was just being paranoid again.

"So what about the activities?" Will asked. "What are they supposed to do for the kids?"

"The idea is that through the activities we give them positive, happy memories to connect to what could otherwise be a very difficult time."

"I guess that makes sense. But what about missing school?"

"Well, most of our intensive family sessions run in the summer. Throughout the year we have shorter, one- to two-week sessions to coincide with school vacations. We also have longer adult-only sessions several times a year."

"As the children's activities director, what do you do during the sessions with no kids?"

"There's always work to be done, new activities to plan. Sometimes I help out the other counselors. I keep myself busy."

"But you live here year round."

"Yep. This is my home." Even more than that, it was her refuge from the harsh world she'd once known. A place that she never wanted to return to, that she never wanted her son exposed to.

"Don't you ever wish for a normal life?"

Normal? She didn't even know what that was. "Define *normal*. The way I was raised was far from 'normal' by most people's standards. For me, this *is* normal now."

"You don't get tired of it?"

"Of what?"

"Dealing with damaged people. Listening to the same problems over and over. It seems like it would get…depressing."

"It can at times. But I feel like I'm doing a lot of good here. That's important to me."

"It must keep you busy. I haven't seen much of you the past couple of days."

It might have been her imagination, but he sounded disappointed. "The first week is always a little crazy. We had a counselor leave due to a family emergency Monday, and her replacement arrived recently. That should lighten my load a bit."

"I looked for you at dinner last night. I was hoping we could eat together again. When you weren't there, I thought you might be avoiding me."

There was no mistaking the disappointment that time. "Adam and I ate in our cabin. I try at least a couple of times a week to make dinner. It's our special time together. And then there are the times when I'm so exhausted I don't even want to think about cooking. In that case, it's just easier to eat in the dining room."

"I imagine you don't get a lot of time with him."

"As much as any working mother gets with her child. As children's activities director, I have the luxury of stopping in and seeing him anytime I want during the day."

"He's a cute kid. He looks just like you."

Abi couldn't help wondering if he'd meant that as a compliment to her or if she was just reading too much into his words, seeing things that weren't really there.

As they neared the main building, their steps slowed.

"I take it he doesn't see his father," Will said.

"He's dead."

"I'm sorry."

"Don't be. He wouldn't have been much of a father anyway. Everything worked out for the best."

"How would he feel about you raising his son in this environment?"

She frowned. "What environment?"

"I just doesn't seem very…stable. What about friends?"

"He has friends. He meets new children all time."

"And in a week or a month they're gone. That can't be healthy. What does he do when there are no kids here? Doesn't he get lonely?"

Abi didn't appreciate his tone or his questioning her abilities as a parent. It was none of his business. Besides, she and Adam were doing just fine. He was happy and well-adjusted. "I don't need to justify my decisions to you or anyone else."

She was right. And besides, what did Will care how she raised her kid? It wasn't his problem. In a few weeks he would be gone and he would never see them again.

But for some reason he did care and he couldn't make himself shut up. He knew he was making her angry, but that remnant of his old man he'd never quite shaken off had reared its ugly head, and it was tough to beat it back down. "It just doesn't seem fair to the kid. I grew up moving from military base to military base. It seemed like every time I made friends we were transferred somewhere else. It's no way to grow up."

"Until you've had kids, do not preach to me about what makes good parenting." She looked at her watch. "I have to get back to work. Thanks for helping me with Eric and Leanne."

"Abi—"

"I'll see you around."

He watched her walk away, shaking his head.

Stupid, stupid, stupid.

He'd made some really good progress; now he was back to square one. All that mattered was finding Ryan's killer, and he'd let his damned pride cloud his vision.

What had he expected her to do? Agree with him and admit she was a lousy parent? Thank him for showing her the error of her ways?

She was right, it was none of his business.

Maybe it was the memory of his own childhood that was the real issue. Always moving, forever feeling like the outsider. Maybe it had hurt him more than he'd realized and more than he wanted to admit. As he'd gotten older he'd learned to compensate, to get the attention he'd craved by being a class clown. He was sure Adam would adjust, too, in his own way. And someday Abi might move on. She couldn't stay in a place like this forever. She might meet a man and get married. Anything could happen, and it wasn't fair of him to stick his nose in where it didn't belong.

He wasn't the apologizing type. He'd always had a problem admitting he was wrong—another cast-off trait from his father. But if he was going to get back into her good graces, get to Maureen through her, he was going to have to do just that.

Even more importantly, he owed it to her.

"What do you mean you don't know?" Vince Collucci paced the carpet in front of the window of his penthouse apartment. The lights from the casino across the street reflected off the blinds, flashing a kaleidoscope of color across his face.

He could feel the beginnings of a migraine and snapped the blinds shut. "You have the picture. Either it's her or it isn't," he said into the phone.

"That's the thing. I don't know what she looks like."

Vince ground his teeth, felt his eyeballs throb. "You're family, Mikey, and I love you like a brother, but my patience is wearing thin."

"I'm tellin' ya, Vince, I really can't see her. She's got this apartment or somethin' in the main building and she never comes out."

"So go in and get her."

"The place is locked up like freaking Fort Knox and there's security cameras everywhere in the building. I can't get in to see her, Vince. No one can."

"What about Bishop?"

"I don't think he has, either. He's been hanging around with a woman that works here. I think he's using her to get to Crystal."

If the woman hiding there *was* the real Crystal. He'd waited four long years to find her, the money-grubbing bitch. She would pay for stealing from him, for turning him over to the feds. "Bishop isn't stupid. If he thinks this woman can get him inside, she probably can. You stick to him like glue and you find a way in. The minute you know anything, you call me."

"I will Vince, I promise."

"But you do not kill her, you understand? I've been looking forward to that for too long."

"I know, Vince, I know."

"Is something bothering you, Abi?"

Abi looked up to see Maureen carrying two cups of coffee to the table and realized she'd zoned out again. All through dinner her mind had kept wandering, drifting up into the ozone somewhere. It wasn't like her to be so…flighty. But she knew exactly what the problem was. Ever since her conversation with Will that afternoon, the only thing she could think about was her son.

She glanced over at him, sprawled on the floor in front of Maureen's big-screen television, his eyes glued to a cartoon. He looked happy and acted happy, but what if that changed? What if a time came that they had to leave? Where would she go? What would she do? She was no stranger to taking care of herself. She'd been on her own for a long time. She'd always managed to keep her head above water. Now it was different. Now she had someone else to care for, another life she was responsible for. The idea of making a mistake scared her to death.

"Abi?" Maureen asked, concern in her voice.

She turned to Maureen and forced a smile. "No, I'm fine. Just a little tired. You know how the first week can be."

Maureen set the coffees down and slid into the chair across from Abi, folding her legs underneath her. "How's it going so far? Have you made much progress with Eric?"

Abi sipped her coffee, the hot cup warming her cold hands. "It's going slowly, but he is opening up a little. Leanne Sanders seems to have a bit of a crush on him, so I sort of set the two up this afternoon."

Maureen's eyebrows rose. "Matchmaking, Abi?"

Will had asked her the same thing. "Not exactly. I thought they each could use a friend to help them open up."

"Leanne? She's the one who's here with her father and sister?"

"That's her."

"From what I understand, the girl's mother was always something of a free spirit. Apparently she took off with her personal assistant."

"I'd heard something like that." Despite strict rules about personal privacy, people talked and information spread. It was inevitable. "I take it he was younger?"

"*She* was younger."

Abi cringed. "Now that I *hadn't* heard."

Maureen sighed. "After doing this for three years, nothing surprises me anymore."

"Do you ever get...I don't know...*tired* of it? Tired of the dysfunction?"

"Of course I do."

"Do you see yourself still doing this ten years from now?"

"I'm not sure. A lot can happen in ten years."

She found herself asking the same questions Will had asked her, though when he'd asked, it had felt almost condescending—like a slight on her career, her decisions. But there was so much he didn't know, didn't understand. "Do you ever question your life? Ever think you made a mistake hiding out like this?"

"Of course I do, Abi. Everyone questions their decisions. Sometimes I get tired of the isolation. Then I think of what life would be like if my identity got out." She shook her head. She was nearly the same age as Abi, but sometimes she got a certain look in her eyes, a sadness that made her look years older. The things she'd been through, Abi couldn't even imagine. It made her own life look like a picnic. "I'm just not ready to deal with that part of my life yet."

"But someday you will?"

"I can't hide forever. Until then, I know I'm doing a lot of good here." She reached across the table and slid her hand over Abi's. "Are you sure you're okay?"

"I just...someone said something to me earlier today and it got me thinking. I've made so many mistakes—"

"Everyone makes mistakes, Abi."

"Lately I feel like...like I'm in limbo. I used to have

a plan. I used to know exactly what I was going to do and how I was going to do it, but it feels as if I've been flung off course somehow."

"Things never seem to work out the way we plan them to, do they?"

"So what now? Come up with a new plan? Wait it out and see what happens?"

Maureen squeezed her hand. "You're my best counselor and more importantly you're my friend. I don't know how I would run this place without you and I would miss you terribly if you left, but if you feel it's time to move on, I'll understand."

It amazed her sometimes the way Maureen understood her. Sometimes better than she understood herself. "You've done so much for me. You saved my life."

"Eventually everyone has to face their past."

Maybe that was what all this indecision, all this second-guessing herself, boiled down to—the idea of facing her past. Like Maureen, she knew someday it would come out. Someday she would have to deal with the things she'd done and make amends.

"But when?" she asked Maureen. "When do you know if it's the right time?"

"I can't tell you that. No one can. When you're ready, you'll just know."

Chapter 6

Abi had just put the finishing touches on the spaghetti dinner she'd prepared—Adam's favorite—when she heard a loud rap on their cabin door. She turned the heat off under the mixed veggies, headed for the door and through the screen saw Will standing there. She hadn't spoken to him the rest of the afternoon yesterday and had avoided him all day today.

"Can we talk?" he asked.

She gazed at him through the mesh but didn't open the door. "Now isn't a good time."

"I know you're mad at me—"

"It's not that," she said, even though it was at least part of her reason. "We were just sitting down to dinner."

"I'll only take a minute, I promise."

Glancing back to be sure Adam was still in his room, she stepped out on the porch, folding her arms across the red faculty T-shirt she hadn't yet changed out of. "Okay."

"I'm here to say I'm sorry for the way I acted the other day. I had no right to judge you or question the way you're raising your son. It's none of my business and it was wrong of me. I have no excuse other than to say I can be overbearing and opinionated sometimes."

"So I've noticed."

He jammed his hands in his pockets, looking sullen and remorseful, but he met her eyes. "It's something I'm trying very hard to change. I hope you'll accept my apology and not let my behavior get in the way of our friendship."

The last thing she needed was an overbearing, opinionated man in her life. She didn't need friends that badly. The problem was, he really did look sorry and he'd gone out of his way to apologize to her, which meant he probably did want to change. She knew how difficult it could be to admit your own faults. She had as many as the next woman.

What kind of person would she be if she didn't accept his apology? If she held a grudge? She probably shouldn't have been so harsh in the first place. If they were really going to try to be friends, she should simply tell him when he did something that upset or offended her. How else would he learn to change his behavior?

"I accept your apology," she said. "And I apologize, too. If I was angry, I should have confronted you about it. I'm always telling people to talk their problems through, yet I have a terrible habit of bottling things up inside. It's something *I'd* like to change."

"I'd appreciate it if you tell me when I do something stupid. I have a really tough time saying I'm sorry, so the fewer mistakes I make, the better." Will grinned, and she couldn't help returning his smile.

"I think that's just a guy thing," she said. "I don't know if I've ever met a man who liked apologizing."

"I'm glad we can still be friends." He took her hand and gave it a squeeze, his palm warm and a little rough, and shivers of sensation shimmied all the way up her arm. Then their eyes locked and held. There was so much sincerity in his, she felt a little choked up. The truth is, she'd felt miserable all day thinking their friendship had ended before it had a chance to bloom. She didn't know why she liked Will so much, why she cared.

She just did.

He glanced behind him to the path, breaking the spell. He dropped her hand and tucked his own back into the pocket of his shorts. "Well, I'll let you get back to your dinner before it gets cold."

She didn't have a second to think before the next words popped out of her mouth. "Would you like to stay and have dinner with us?"

"Are you sure? I know this is your special time with Adam. I don't want to interfere." Will should have jumped at the chance. The closer he was to her, the sooner he would get to Maureen. He just couldn't help feeling guilty, as if he were deceiving her somehow. The truth was, he wanted to be her friend. He'd felt like a first-rate slime for the way he'd treated her yesterday. He wasn't just apologizing because he had to. He really was sorry. And that bit about changing his ways hadn't been a lie.

He was here at Healing Hearts, and it wasn't cheap. He might as well get his money's worth, really make an effort to be a better person.

Abi looked hesitant for a second and then she smiled. "Yeah, I'm sure. Adam would love to have you. He talks about you a lot."

"He does?" She held the door open and he stepped inside the cabin. The interior was much like that in the main building and the guest cabins but with personal touches added. It was warm and cozy and comfortable. And big. At least triple the size of his own cabin.

Abi stepped in behind him and the door creaked shut on squeaky springs. "He has a lot of questions about your face, what you do for a living. He's not entirely convinced you aren't a superhero."

"I wish my life were that exciting," he said.

"Adam!" she called. "Dinnertime. We have a guest."

Adam came bounding out of his bedroom, sliding to a stop when he saw Will. "Hi, Mr. Bishop!"

Will crouched down to say hello. "Hey, Adam."

"You're eating dinner with us?"

"Yep."

"Cool!"

He was so excited, so genuinely happy, Will once again felt that shaft of guilt. He had to remind himself that he'd done nothing wrong. He and Abi were just going to be friends. No harm done.

"Adam, it's okay if you call me Will."

Adam looked up at his mom. "Could I?"

"As long as Will doesn't mind," Abi said. "Now why don't you set an extra place at the table?"

Adam trotted off to the kitchen—he didn't walk so much as bounce—and Will pulled himself to his feet. "Is there anything I can do to help?"

"You can open the wine," she called over her shoulder on her way to the kitchen. "It's on the table."

He found the bottle—a cabernet—and drove the corkscrew into the cork.

"Do you drink wine or would you prefer a beer? I have both." She grabbed two oven mitts from the counter to lift a large pot from the stove and carry it to the table.

"I'm usually a beer drinker, but wine is a nice change every now and then."

"Me, too." She grabbed a second wineglass from the cupboard above the sink and set it at the table.

He poured both glasses as Adam walked slowly to the table, a plate, fork, and knife balanced precariously in his arms.

"How about I give you a hand with those, sport?" Will said.

Adam shot him an indignant look. "I'm not a baby. Setting the table is one of my chores."

He put both hands up in a defensive stance. "My apologies. I've never known a three-year-old who could set a table."

"I'm almost three and a half," Adam said.

Will grinned. "I guess that half a year makes a difference."

Adam set the plate on the table with a thunk, dangerously close to the edge, and Will tried not to cringe when he imagined it dropping to the floor and shattering. The silverware clattered to the table beside it. "See, I know how."

"You sure do."

"Great job, kiddo," Abi said, rumpling his hair. "Now go wash your hands."

If Will hadn't thought Abi was beautiful before, that changed as he watched her with her son. When she looked at Adam, an aura of pure love and happiness glowed around her. He'd never known happiness like that, never known such an unconditional love. Adam was one lucky kid to have a mother like Abi.

Maybe Will had been wrong. Maybe Adam could be content living at the retreat. The kid appeared happy and well-adjusted. So what if it was a little out of the norm. What was normal these days anyway?

When Adam disappeared into the bathroom, Abi slid the plate more securely on the table and arranged the silverware neatly beside it. "He's very independent," she explained. "He looks so proud when he helps me, I figure it's worth a few chipped dishes."

"He seems like a really good kid."

"He is. Don't get me wrong, he has his moments. He can be stubborn and demanding. If he doesn't like the way something is being done, he's not shy about speaking his mind."

Adam bounded back into the room waving his hands in the air. "All clean!"

"Did you use soap?"

"Yup!" He climbed into the chair with the booster seat strapped to it and banged on the table beside him. "Sit by me, Will."

"Demanding, huh?" Will said and Abi smiled.

"A tad, yes."

Will sat in the seat beside Adam and across from Abi. He and Abi scooted their chairs in at the same time and their feet collided under the table. They said, "Sorry" simultaneously, then she laughed nervously and bit her lip. "It's been a while since we had a dinner guest. I mean, we have other staff over all the time. Just not…"

"Strange men?" Will asked.

"Yeah," she admitted.

"It's a little unusual for me, too," he said. It had been a long time since a relationship with a woman had resulted in a shared home-cooked meal. Generally he took women out to eat. He liked to keep the playing ground neutral. If dinner went well, they might end up back at her place or on rare occasions in a hotel. He didn't bring women to his apartment. He didn't give out his home number either, only his cell. He liked to be in control at all times, keep the upper hand in a relationship, in the event a quick escape was needed.

"We hafta say grace," Adam said, holding out his hands for Will and Abi to take. "Or God will make the food taste bad."

Will gave Abi a questioning look.

"Last session Adam ate dinner with a family who said grace before every meal. He decided he and I should do it, too. I hope you don't mind."

"Of course not." He folded Adam's small, slightly damp hand in his own. "I was raised Catholic."

"And I didn't see the inside of a church until a friend of mine got married. And that was a Vegas chapel, so it probably doesn't even count."

The call they'd received implicating Vince Collucci in Ryan's death had originated from Vegas. Will wondered if that was where Abi had met Maureen.

He filed away the information for later.

"Mommy," Adam groaned. "You and Will gotta hold hands, too, or God won't hear."

"Sorry, I forgot."

Will reached across the table to take Abi's outstretched hand and saw that she was actually blushing. She always seemed a bit uneasy when he touched her. Maybe she just wasn't used to the physical contact.

He, on the other hand, relished it. Probably due to a lack of it in his childhood. When his father hadn't been around, his mother had hugged and kissed him, but when his old man had been home—which had been most of the time since he'd retired when Will was ten— she hadn't dared. Physical affection hadn't been tolerated. It turned boys into sissies, he'd said. In all the years his parents were married Will had never seen them kiss or embrace. They'd never even held hands.

"Now you gotta close your eyes," Adam instructed. He closed his eyes, lowered his head and said in an earnest voice, "Dear God, thank you for the spaghetti. It's my favorite. Amen."

Both Abi and Will said amen, then she dished out the food. If Will had thought he and Abi would have a chance to talk during the meal, he'd been wrong. Adam chattered nonstop. He talked about his new friends, the project they had done in art that afternoon, the picnic they'd had on the beach. He told Will about the counselors and how Susie in the office always gave him a piece of candy and that Maureen had a huge TV with Nickelodeon.

Adam seemed to know a little bit about everyone and was brutally honest. A few times Abi scolded him for revealing things he'd heard people say—private things Will was sure had never been meant for his ears, but the kid didn't seem to miss a thing. He was like a sponge. Will wondered if he might be able to get some information about Maureen from Adam, then instantly felt guilty for the thought. Pumping a three-year-old for information was low even for him. He wasn't that desperate. Not yet. But if Adam just happened to mention something and Will were to inquire further, that might be different.

After dinner Will helped them clear the table and then they sat on the big fluffy rug in front of the couch and played Go Fish. He'd always imagined hanging out with a woman and her kid would be domestic torture. Instead he found himself having a good time. It was…fun, even though Will was pretty sure Adam was cheating. The kid was destined to be a card shark some day.

At nine, when Abi told Adam it was time to get ready for bed, Will almost felt disappointed.

"We have company, so only one book tonight," she told Adam.

"I want Will to read to me," Adam demanded.

Abi frowned. "Adam, I don't think—"

"*Pleeease,*" Adam begged and turned to Will, a pleading look in his eyes. "Can you?"

"I'll read you a book," Will heard himself saying.

Adam started hopping up and down. "Yeah!"

Abi gave him a playful swat on the behind. "Go brush your teeth and get your pj's on, monkey boy." When he'd hopped out of the room, she turned to Will. "I'm sorry he put you on the spot like that. You don't have to read to him if you don't want to."

"I don't mind," he said and realized he meant it. And not just because he thought he had something to gain. He wasn't even sure why. It just seemed the appropriate way to end the evening.

"He's really been craving male attention lately. He's just beginning to question why he doesn't have a daddy." She gathered the cards and stood. "It's confusing for him."

"I understand." He stood and tossed the pillows they'd been leaning on back on the couch. "If you'd prefer I didn't read to him, it won't hurt my feelings."

She wasn't sure how she felt about it. Adam was at an impressionable age. Not that she thought Will would be a bad influence. It was just that since meeting Will in the dining room the other night, Adam had become oddly fascinated with him. He'd asked her a million questions about him, things Abi couldn't answer. Things she wondered herself.

She was afraid if Adam knew too much, he might become too attached to Will. Even more than that, *she* didn't want to become attached. Though the meal they'd shared couldn't have been more casual and she'd played Go Fish with Adam a thousand times, there was something so intimate about the three of them spending time together. Maybe because it was a first for her. Adam's father had been out of the picture long before Adam had been born, and Abi never knew her own father. The men her mother had brought home and the ones she'd married weren't the type to sit down for a family dinner, even if her mom had known how to cook anything more complicated than frozen dinners.

But if it made Adam happy, what harm could one little story do? She would just make it very clear to Adam tomorrow that Will was only a friend. And like all the other guests, he would be leaving and they would probably never see him again.

"I think he'd like it a lot if you read to him," she told Will.

"You're sure?"

She smiled. "I'm sure."

"I'm ready!" Adam called from his bedroom doorway. They both turned to find him standing there in his short-sleeved superhero pajamas. Since meeting Will they were the only ones he would wear.

That seed of doubt pushed just a little closer to the surface. It seemed that all she did lately was question herself. This time she would just have to follow her instincts and hope she didn't make a mistake.

"Would you like me to tuck you in?" she asked.

"Nope. Will can do it."

She propped her hands on her hips and said sternly, "I at least get a kiss, don't I?"

He scurried into the room and gave her a quick kiss—so quick his lips didn't even hit their target—then he grabbed Will's hand and dragged him toward his bedroom. 'C'mon!"

While Will read to Adam, Abi kept herself busy washing the dinner dishes. She stopped briefly and peeked around the corner toward Adam's room. She couldn't see them, but she could hear the deep rumble of Will's voice. Then his tone rose to an unnaturally high pitch, and she realized he was changing his voice to represent the different characters. She heard Adam giggle and she smiled. Then something in her heart, an emotion that was too familiar, had tears burning in the corners of her eyes.

She felt…cheated.

Cheated out of a father and a "normal" life, a conventional family. Maybe this was her punishment for all of her sins. And her son—was he destined to feel cheated, too?

She swallowed the plug of emotion in her throat, wiped away the moisture overflowing from her eyes, then dried the clean dishes and put them away. She was setting the last plate in the cupboard when Will appeared in the kitchen doorway.

"That was a long book," she said.

"Three and a half books," Will said with a grin. "He went out like a light halfway through book number four."

"*Four* books? Either you're really nice or extremely gullible."

"Gullible, I think." He lifted the wine bottle from the counter. "How about one more glass?"

She glanced at the clock and wondered fleetingly what the other staff members would think if they knew she'd had a retreat guest in her cabin past nine-thirty—or that she'd had one there at all. Then she decided right now she didn't care what anyone thought. They weren't doing anything wrong, anything inappropriate.

"I'd love one," she said and watched as Will emptied the bottle into their glasses. He handed one to her and she took a long swallow, the full-bodied liquid making a warm path all the way down. She never had more than two glasses of wine at one sitting. This being her third, she began to get a mellow, languid feeling in her belly. "Why don't we sit on the couch?"

"Sounds good to me," Will agreed.

She sat with her legs curled under her, and Will settled beside her, his long, tanned legs stretched out in front of him. She wondered absently what it would feel like to touch him, to run her hand up his thigh, through the coarse hair, underneath the leg of his shorts.

The direction of her thoughts startled her. What on earth had made her think such a thing? In the past, she had only ever been with a man because it served a purpose. She had nothing to gain from Will. No reason to seduce him. Besides, it had been so long since she'd touched a man, so long since she'd felt the need, she wondered if she would even remember how. Yet her fingers itched to try, so she curled her hand into a tight fist instead.

Will took a sip from his glass, and she watched the muscles in his throat work as he swallowed. His neck was lean and muscled like the rest of him. His face was long and narrow with a hint of dark stubble on his chin and cheek, his mouth wide and inviting, with one corner pulled up into a grin. Her gaze traveled up to the narrow blade of his nose and the eyes that were not quite brown, not quite green.

The eyes looking right back at her.

She realized with dismay that she'd been caught staring again and lowered her eyes to her lap.

"The way you look at me sometimes…" Will said. "What is it you find so fascinating about my face?"

She felt her cheeks fill with heat. "Sorry."

"Don't apologize. I'm not saying that to tease you. I'm really curious."

She looked up and realized he was serious.

"Is it the scars?"

That wasn't it at all. "The truth is, I don't even notice your scars anymore."

One brow rose with skepticism. "How can you not notice them?"

"They're just a part of your face, I guess. Like your nose or your chin."

He turned his body toward her, his knee brushing against her bare leg, and suddenly they were sitting much closer. Closer than she'd sat with a man in a very long time.

He rested one arm on the back of the couch between them. "So what is it? Why do you look at me that way?"

"What way?"

"Like you're trying to figure me out."

Maybe she was. Maybe she was trying to figure out

what it was about him that drew her in, what made her want to look. And keep looking.

She took another gulp of wine. The warm feeling spread to her fingers and toes and made her head feel fuzzy. "I find your face very…interesting."

The corner of his mouth quirked up. "Not attractive, not devastatingly handsome. Just…interesting?"

"You don't need me to tell you that you're handsome."

"Don't I?"

She should have been embarrassed, but the wine was making her feel bold. She looked him square in the eye and said, "You know you are."

Their eyes locked and held. "Why don't you tell me anyway."

She used to be a master at seduction, at vocal foreplay. Knowing she could slip so easily back into the role, that a few glasses of wine could lower her defenses, frightened and excited her all at once. She'd missed this feeling of sexual power. She'd missed it almost as much as it scared her. She'd been suppressing these urges and feelings for so long, finally setting them loose made her feel…free.

He reached up and brushed her cheek lightly with the tips of his fingers. Her skin tingled where he touched her, but she didn't pull away. She wanted him to touch her. They were close, as close as they'd been the night he'd walked her home, when he'd put her hand on his face and she'd wanted so badly to kiss him. The way she did now.

"You're beautiful," he said, stroking her cheek, her

chin, her lower lip, making her feel weak and shaky with arousal.

But she wasn't beautiful. Not physically anyway. Not anymore. There had been a time when she could stop men cold with her looks. But her soul, that had been dark and ugly. The soul was what mattered. Being beautiful on the inside.

Maybe that was what he saw.

His eyes searched her face. "You confuse the hell out of me, Abi."

That made two of them, because she was feeling pretty confused right now, too. Everything in her screamed that this was a bad idea. He was a guest, he was twice divorced, not to mention probably in desperate need of the therapy he refused to participate in. And still she wanted to kiss him.

She didn't just want it, she *craved* it. She'd never desired a man the way she did Will. Maybe she'd never let herself.

Now wasn't the time to break that tradition.

"I don't understand how a woman so sweet and unassuming can be so damned sexy. It's like you're two different people."

She *was* two people, and her other self, the one she'd buried four years ago, was suddenly clawing to get out. But somehow this was different. She wanted nothing from him, had no ulterior motives. This was sexual attraction at its purest, even though what she was feeling right now was anything but pure. In fact, she was feeling downright naughty.

His head tipped to one side and she knew he was

going to kiss her. She didn't care. She wanted him to kiss her.

His fingers slipped across her cheek, into her hair, his eyes searching her face. "If you don't tell me to stop, I'm going to kiss you."

She couldn't make her mouth form the word. Instead she leaned forward, meeting him halfway, until their lips touched. The kiss was gentle at first, barely a whisper, then his mouth rubbed sensuously against hers, tempting her, coaxing her to open up to him. He tasted like wine and passion and something undeniably exciting. Something wild and reckless and dangerous.

His tongue rubbed softly and slowly against her own in a hypnotizing rhythm. She felt the contours of his face in her hands and realized she was touching him. The puckered skin of one cheek, the raspy roughness of the other. Her fingers took on a will of their own, exploring, discovering. She touched his cheeks, smoothed her thumbs over the creases at the corners of his eyes. She felt his hand cup her check, the other tangle in her hair as he urged her closer.

She curled her hands over his shoulders. His skin felt hot underneath the thin cotton shirt. Suddenly a kiss wasn't enough. She wanted to touch him, to be touched. She wanted to feel bare skin and lean muscle. She felt herself leaning closer, melting into him—

"Mommy!"

Through a sexual fog she heard her son's sleepy, frightened cry. The thought of Adam seeing her and Will this way, the confusion it could cause, was like a blast of icy water.

Will must have felt it, too, because he pulled away the exact second she did.

"Mommy!" Adam called again more urgently, and Abi realized he must still be in bed. At least he hadn't seen them and she wouldn't have to explain. If he had, it would have been a disaster. He would have been so confused and, chatterbox that he could be, might have told one of the staff. Or all of them.

Abi rose from the couch, her legs feeling wobbly, her brain slightly fuzzy. "I have to…"

Will nodded, looking nearly as guilty as she felt. "Go ahead."

"Give me a minute. Then we'll talk."

Chapter 7

Will filled his lungs with cool, dry night air, trying to slow the pounding of his heart. He hadn't come here planning to kiss her, but now that he had, he wanted more. When he'd imagined kissing her, he'd thought she would be shy and maybe a little awkward. Instead she'd melted against him, their bodies fitting together naturally, as if one had been built with the other in mind. A perfect compliment.

He closed his eyes, let the darkness swallow him up.

He didn't want to feel this way about Abi. Considering the nature of his business at the retreat, things could get complicated if he let this go any further. For four years he'd been working to bring Ryan's killer to justice. He couldn't let himself get distracted now. His own happiness, his own fulfillment, were the last things on his mind.

At least, they should have been.

Behind him he heard the door hinges squeak. Abi stepped outside and joined him on the porch. "There you are. I though maybe you got tired of waiting and left."

They both knew that wouldn't be his reason for leaving. But he wasn't the type to run away when confronted with a dilemma.

"Adam had a nightmare," she said.

"Is he okay?"

"Fine. It happens every now and then. I sat with him for a few minutes and he fell right back to sleep."

He turned to her, just barely able to make out her features in the pale light streaming through the screen door. "About what happened—"

"It was my fault," Abi said.

He hadn't expected her to take responsibility for something that was clearly *his* fault. "It's not your fault."

"No, it is. I've been sending you mixed signals all night. Between the dinner and the cards and the wine…tonight was really nice. The truth is, I just got caught up in the moment."

"I guess I did, too," he admitted. He hadn't had such a good time since…well, he couldn't even remember when. He'd really never had an experience like the one he'd just had with Abi.

Over the past four years it was as if all the flavor in his life, the passion for anything but justice, was gone. When he was with Abi, he tasted life again. "I don't know why I kissed you. I mean, I know *why,* I just…

I apologize if I…" He raked a hand through his hair. "Hell, I don't know what I'm trying to say. I should say I'm sorry, but the truth is, I'm not. I'd probably do it again if I thought you would let me."

Abi was grinning.

"You think I'm an idiot, don't you?"

She shook her head. "No, you're just always so in control. It's kind of cute to see you flustered."

"I'm glad I've been entertaining."

"You know anything other than a friendship would be a bad idea," Abi said. "For both of us."

"Because it's against the rules?"

"Because I have a three-year-old son. I don't get the luxury of having a fling. Even if I did, that isn't the kind of person I am."

"Flings are all I have," he admitted. "That *is* the kind of person I am."

She leaned against the porch railing and folded her arms across her chest. "Why do you suppose that is?"

"Are you shrinking me?"

Abi grinned. "Not my field of expertise. I'm just curious."

"I know exactly why. I'm no good at relationships. I was a lousy husband. After my second divorce I decided I wasn't cut out for marriage."

"Then why come here?"

Good question. One he couldn't answer without lying, and he didn't want to lie to Abi. He went for evasion instead. "When I figure that out, I'll let you know."

"Fair enough." She looked into the cabin, then back at Will. "It's getting late. I have an early start tomorrow."

"Will I see you at breakfast?"

"Most mornings I skip breakfast in the dining room and take an hour hike."

"I like to hike. Maybe I could join you."

She thought about it for a minute, then a smile curled her mouth. "On one condition. You have to go to group therapy first."

He winced. "That's blackmail."

"Yeah, it is," she agreed. "But if you really want to hike with me, you'll have to do it."

"It's a free country. I could just show up at your cabin in the morning and follow you."

"You could, but you won't."

Damned if she wasn't right. If he did, that would only make her angry, and he didn't want to tick her off. He couldn't let himself forget he needed her to get to Maureen. "Okay, no hiking. But can we at least have lunch together?"

"Lunch would be nice." She edged toward the door. "But consider the therapy. You might change your mind."

"I doubt it."

She smiled. "I'll see you tomorrow."

She stepped into the cabin, shutting the wood door behind her. When he heard the dead bolt snap, he turned and walked down the path. It was so dark, he could see little more than shadowy shapes and he had the eerie feeling he was being watched. He'd felt the same way earlier in the week, when he was at the beach. He'd thought for sure it was Abi watching him, since she tended to do that, but when he'd looked around, he hadn't seen her anywhere.

He was sure it was just a trick of his mind. What reason would anyone have for watching him? No one knew who he really was.

At least, he hoped they didn't.

Will walked into his cabin the exact second his cell phone began to ring. He closed and locked the door, then pulled it from the pocket of his shorts. "Bishop."

"It's Robbins. Can you talk?"

He was exhausted and the last thing he felt like doing was giving the assistant director an update on his progress—or lack thereof. This was not a bureau-sanctioned investigation, so technically he didn't have to tell him squat. On the other hand, if it weren't for Robbins, Will might not be here at all.

He collapsed on the sofa, put his feet on the coffee table and said, "Yeah, I can talk."

"We might have a problem."

Oh, swell. Like he didn't have enough already. "What kind of problem?"

"There's been some interesting information coming from the Sardoni wiretaps. Three times over the past two weeks Colorado was mentioned."

Will sat up, his feet hitting the wood floor with a thud. It could mean nothing or it could mean the Sardonis were onto him.

Damn, damn, damn.

"Why am I just hearing about this now?"

"Because *I* just heard about it. No one knows you're there. They had no reason to bring it to my attention."

His tone was grim. "I think the Sardonis suspect what you're doing."

Will cursed under his breath. "How could they even know I'm here?"

"If you're thinking I told someone, I haven't. It's no secret you're hot to get Vince. All I can figure is they've got someone keeping tabs on you."

Which was actually good news. "If they had eliminated her, they wouldn't be looking, either. So she's definitely alive."

"It could also mean they've sent someone to tail you. Have you noticed anyone suspicious?"

"No one," he said. If someone was there, they'd blended in.

"Did anyone arrive after you?"

"Not that I—wait a minute. There was a replacement counselor that arrived a couple of days after the session started. Tom something." The kid was pretty young, but that didn't mean he wasn't part of the crime family.

"Do you have a last name?"

"No, but I can get one."

"What about the other guests? Can you get me their names?"

There were at least forty. Though half were children, which would narrow the odds considerably. The names of the people he didn't know he might be able to get off the therapy sign-up sheets. He was pretty sure they listed first and last names.

"I'll get a list to you by tomorrow."

"Do it and we'll run background checks. Until then, do you have your sidearm?"

"Of course." Locked up in his suitcase with his identification, where housekeeping wouldn't accidentally
stumble across it.

"Keep it on you."

"Yeah, that's not going to look suspicious."

"I take it you haven't gotten to the owner yet?"

"Not yet. I've been staying close to one of the counselors." He wasn't about to tell Robbins just how close.
"She's good friends with Maureen. I'm hoping she can
get me in to see her."

"What about this counselor? Could she be the one
you're looking for?"

He thought of Abi, tried to picture her with a scum-
bag like Vince. "No, it's definitely not her. She's got a
three-and-a-half-year-old kid. You saw the security
shots. Crystal wasn't pregnant. But Abi did mention
that she used to live in Vegas. I believe that's where she
met Maureen."

"You want me to run her name just in case?"

As an agent, he knew it only made sense to check
her out, but as her friend, it felt like a betrayal. He'd
wanted her to trust him—shouldn't he trust her?

But trust wasn't the only issue here. This was life
or death.

Maybe hers.

Oh, hell. If he was being watched, they might think
that because he'd taken an interest in her, *Abi* was the
one they were looking for. If someone found out they'd
run her name, he could be putting her and her son in
even more danger.

He could try backing off, but if someone *was* at the

retreat watching him, the damage was already done. Either he told her the truth now, which would most surely blow his chance to get to Maureen, or he didn't let her out of his sight.

And how did he plan to do that? She took a hike every morning alone in the woods. It would be the perfect opportunity for someone to grab her. He didn't doubt that whoever might be here hadn't been sent to kill Crystal. Vince would want to do that himself, after he got out of her what happened to his money. And when he found out they had the wrong woman, he would kill her anyway.

The thought made him sick to his stomach.

He could follow Abi through the woods without her knowing, but he would have to stay far enough away so he wouldn't be discovered. Too far to circumvent a possible kidnapping attempt. And if she did see him, found out he was tailing her, she would be fuming mad. He would never get her to introduce him to Maureen.

Christ, this was getting complicated.

The only way to protect her was to hike *with* her. And the only way to do that was to—*ugh*—go to therapy.

What had he gotten himself into?

"It would be a waste of time to run her name," he told Robbins. "It's not her."

"I'll be honest. When you first came to me with this, I thought it was a dead end. Now I might have enough evidence to take this to the director. I could send another agent in."

"There's no way to do that without tipping off the owner that I'm here, and that's the one thing that I *can't* do. I don't doubt she'll disappear again."

"Then I'm going to contact the Denver office and alert them to the situation."

"Don't."

"Bishop, for cryin' out loud—"

"We get agents sniffing around here, Maureen will be gone. I have to do this alone."

He was quiet for several seconds, then said, "You've got a week."

No way he would be getting to Maureen that soon. It just wasn't possible. "I've only been here a week. I need at least two more."

Another pause. Then his boss said, "Get me the names and I'll have them run by Monday or Tuesday. If everyone checks out, you have your two weeks. If anyone looks even marginally suspicious, I'm getting you out of there."

"It's not your call. I'm here on my own, remember?"

"Will, I won't be responsible for losing another one of my best agents. If I were you, I'd find a way to get to the owner and I'd do it fast."

Apparently Will wasn't the only one feeling guilty over Ryan's death. It made sense now why Robbins had cut him so much slack when it came to investigating a case that had been cold for four years.

He wanted to catch Vince as badly as Will did.

"Call me tomorrow with those names. And, Will?"

"Yeah?"

"Watch your back."

* * *

"Okay. *One* therapy session."

Abi turned from the volleyball game she was overseeing to find Will standing behind her. He was dressed in his typical cargo shorts and a T-shirt the same rusty-green as his eyes. "Beg your pardon?"

"I've given it some thought and I decided one therapy session couldn't hurt. One session and we can hike together."

Abi grinned. She'd been hoping he would come around, even if he had done it grudgingly. But one session was nothing. She wasn't letting him off the hook that easily. "One session won't do anything. Five days. Monday to Friday."

His mouth fell open in indignation. "Five days?"

"Then you can hike with me as often as you like."

"Two days," he said.

"No."

He folded his arms across his chest, pulling the sleeves of his T-shirt tight around his biceps. They weren't huge but very nicely defined. In fact, as far as she could tell, he was pleasantly defined just about everywhere.

"Okay, three," he said.

He was also very stubborn. "This is not negotiable, Will. You either do the full five days or you don't go with me."

He thought about it for a minute, then muttered a foul word under his breath. "Fine, I'll do it."

"You won't be sorry."

"So I'll see you tomorrow morning?"

"For?"

"To go hiking."

"One, I don't hike on weekends, and two, you have to go to the five days of therapy first."

He flashed her another indignant look. "You don't trust me?"

Not as far as she could throw him. He was so against it, she didn't doubt he would find any way out of it he could. "There's a session every morning at ten except Sunday. I expect to see your name on the list starting on Monday. And I'm going to check to make sure you went each day, so don't think you can weasel your way out of it."

"Abi!" David, one of the teen counselors, was waving his arms to get her attention. "Someone got pegged!"

Abi looked over to see one of the kids sitting in the sand rubbing his head. Looked as though someone was going to need an ice pack and some TLC. "Duty calls," she told Will, backing away. "I'll see you at lunch?"

"Yeah," he agreed, but he still looked ticked off.

"Oh, don't be so grumpy," she said. "You might like it."

"I'll go," he called after her. "But I'm *not* going to like it."

"Abi, do you have a minute?"

Abi looked up from the computer screen, where she'd been putting the finishing touches to a treasure map for a camping trip next week. Brittney stood in the doorway looking troubled. Which was normal for her.

She was a nice girl and great with the kids, and without her help babysitting Adam, Abi would be lost. She was also a worrier. She had a knack for taking an ordinary situation and turning it into a three-act drama.

And Abi really *didn't* have a minute—or the ten or fifteen it would take to get whatever was bothering Brit off her chest. Despite that, she put her computer into sleep mode and sat back in her chair.

"What's the problem?" She didn't add the *this time* that she was thinking.

"It's Tom, the new counselor."

"What about him?"

"I know it's not my call, but…well…"

Get to the point, Abi urged mentally.

"I just don't think he's working out," Brit said.

"Not working out how?"

"Well, for one, he's lazy. If I didn't nag him constantly to do stuff, he would just sit around or talk to the guests."

"That's odd. Every time I've seen him, he seems to be doing a great job."

"That's the thing. He's only like that when you're *not* around. I left the kids alone with him the other day to make a run to the supply building and when I came back, the kids were running wild and he wasn't even paying attention! When I called his name, he totally ignored me. I had to say it like ten times. He was flirting with some *girl.*"

"What girl?"

"One of the guests. That Cindy girl," Brit said indignantly. "She's always hanging around him, getting in the

way and distracting him from his work. It's totally inappropriate."

And there lies the root of the problem, Abi thought. Brit
was jealous. She wasn't an ugly girl. If Abi had to choose
a word to describe her it would probably be...*drab*. She
was a little on the pudgy side and had a moderately bad
case of acne. Cindy, on the other hand, had the kind of
exotic beauty that naturally drew the opposite sex.

Maybe Brit liked Tom and resented that he didn't
return the feelings.

"Brit, you know that we thoroughly check out each
applicant before we hire anyone. Tom has impeccable
references. We were very lucky to get him."

Brit shrugged. "I don't know what to tell you, Abi.
He's just not working out."

And obviously Brit wasn't going to back down.

"Tell you what. I'll have a talk with him. In a week,
if you're still having a problem, we'll figure out what
we need to do."

Brit didn't look happy, but she nodded, then turned
and left.

Poor kid. She felt bad for Brit, but she couldn't fire
someone on the grounds of a wounded ego. She made
a mental note to talk to Tom about it in a way that
wouldn't embarrass Brit further.

At times she felt like a referee. It wasn't unusual for
the counselors to get into tiffs every now and then.
Sometimes it was like living in a soap opera. She'd
even broken up a catfight or two in her three years.

But she was sure as always everything would work
out.

Chapter 8

Will crouched behind a tree several hundred yards from the narrow trail, catching his breath and watching as Abi made her way back down the incline that would take her out of the forest. He slapped at the mosquito chewing on his neck and wiped away the sweat rolling down the side of his face.

Doing this for a week was going to be a lot tougher than he'd thought. This was no leisurely stroll she took. She moved with swift efficiency and determination. He considered himself in supreme physical condition and still had trouble keeping up with her. Doing it quietly and off a path of any kind was another issue altogether.

The forest floor was a complicated maze of dried twigs, fallen logs and ratty underbrush. He'd tripped at least a dozen times, fallen twice and three times he'd almost lost sight of her. If it hadn't been for her bright yellow T-shirt, it would have been impossible to track her.

Soon, when she was close enough to the main building to make it safely the rest of the way, he would break off and head back to his cabin for a shower. Already he could hear sounds of civilization, people leaving the dining room and heading to various activities. Through the trees he could see flashes of the maintenance building roof.

He started to move, then heard a noise from behind him—the crunch of twigs snapping. He stopped and listened but heard only silence. Probably just an animal, he decided. A few times during the hike he'd heard noises and had seen nothing. Probably just his mind playing tricks on him again.

He began slowly making his way down a steep decline and he heard it again, unmistakable footsteps. He spun around and through the dense foliage saw movement. Movement too large to be an animal.

Someone was out there.

Heart pounding, he started to back up but lost his footing and slid several feet down through slimy decaying leaves and mud and landed on his rear end. He cursed and pushed himself to his feet, but by the time he regained his footing and looked around, whoever it was had disappeared. He turned and searched for Abi, but she was gone, too.

Damn it.

All weekend he'd kept Abi in his sights—close enough to keep an eye on her but not so close that she mistook him for a stalker—and he hadn't noticed anyone acting suspiciously or hanging around her too much. No one besides him, that is.

Now there was no doubt—someone had been following either him or Abi.

Robbins was supposed to call that evening with whatever information he'd obtained from the names Will had given him. Will hoped he found something so he could quietly remove whomever was shadowing them.

Before someone was hurt.

Two and a half hours later Will sat in the circle of chairs within the small group of men and women— eight including himself—feeling like a complete and total idiot. This therapy thing was so not him, but he didn't exactly have a choice.

"Group, we have a new member," Eve, the therapist announced, then smiled at Will. "Why don't you introduce yourself?"

Oh, jeez. "My name is Will Bishop."

"Hi, Will," the group said in unison, and he nearly choked. It was like every cliché he'd ever seen on television.

"Why don't you tell us a little bit about yourself?"

"Like what?" he asked and prayed silently, *God, please get me the hell out of here.*

"Where you're from, what you do for a living."

"I live in New York and I work for the government."

Eve watched him expectantly. "And…"

Will shrugged. "And that's about it."

"Divorced? In the process of?"

"Divorced," he said, then added, "twice." And got a collective "oh" from the others.

"I just divorced wife number five," one of the men, Larry, told him. Will had played golf with him once and he seemed like a decent guy. Though Will had to wonder what sane man would get married five times.

"Don't you mean *bimbo* number five?" one of the women said bitterly. She appeared to be in her midthirties, but her face looked haggard and tired. She was petite, blond and angry. *Really* angry.

"Claire," Eve said in a patient tone, "remember what we talked about? We're here to help each other, not condemn."

"Her husband left her for a younger woman," Larry told Will, then turned to Claire. "Can I help it if I like 'em young?"

"They're not young," Claire shot back. "They're toddlers."

"Why do you suppose it is that you gravitate toward younger women?" Eve asked Larry.

Larry shrugged. "Do I need a reason?"

"Classic midlife crisis," Jade, a guest that Will had met at the beach, said. She was tall and slender and wore long, flowing, colorful clothing. She was quiet and serene and always looked as if she were either at peace with the world or taking heavy doses of Valium. "It's your way of trying to hang on to your youth," she said calmly. "But the truth is, it only makes you feel older."

"These women who steal husbands are a bunch of

bloodsucking, gold-digging vampires," Claire said, her voice quivering with bottled anger.

"Oh, please," the third woman said indignantly. She was younger. Young enough to be one of those vampires Claire was referring to. "You're just angry because you couldn't hold on to your husband."

"So, Carla," Eve said, "you think Jade and Claire are being unfair?"

It went on like that for the next hour and fifteen minutes. Will just sat back and listened. He had to admit it was interesting, but he didn't feel as if he had anything to contribute or anything in common with these people. He knew exactly what his problem was and he'd fixed it: he was a lousy husband, which he could avoid by not getting married again. Pretty simple.

But being here was his only way to keep Abi safe.

If they had been in a different situation, he might have dated Abi a few times, then brushed her off— especially when he found out she had a son. He wouldn't have given their relationship—friendship or otherwise—a chance to develop.

Now he wanted to know what made her tick, what caused this desire to be close to her, why he'd kissed her when his conscience told him it was wrong and why he couldn't stop thinking about kissing her again.

After the session Will headed to the dining room for lunch. As he cleared the doorway, he gazed around and found exactly what he was looking for—Abi sitting alone at a table near the back.

When she didn't have her son, she always sat alone.

He wondered why. She must be friends with the staff. Why did she seclude herself?

When his eyes landed on her, as if sensing she was being watched, she looked up. He didn't get the usual wary look from her. This time she flashed him a timid smile, and damn, she was pretty. He wondered if there would ever come a time when she didn't seem afraid of him. Well, Friday night she hadn't appeared wary of him at all, but he thought that had a lot more to do with the wine than their developing friendship. He wondered what had happened to her to make her so guarded, so distrustful. Who had hurt her and what had they done to make her so withdrawn and timid?

It was a trait Adam apparently hadn't inherited. The terms *withdrawn* and *timid* factored nowhere into his personality. All weekend the kid had followed Will around, talking a million miles an hour. Before his time with Ryan's family, Will had never considered himself a kid person. Now he didn't mind so much. Not that he was in a rush to run out and have any. But Adam was a nice kid, and being around him had made it easier for Will to stay close to his mother.

Will fixed himself a plate and headed over to Abi's table. Without asking, he pulled out the chair across from her.

"So," she asked before his butt even hit the seat, "how did it go?"

"How did what go?" he asked, though he knew exactly what she meant.

She gave him an impatient look. "The *therapy.*"

"Oh, that," he said casually. He draped his napkin in his lap. "It was…interesting."

She looked pleased. "That's a start, I guess."

She'd checked the list that morning and after seeing his name, had peeked into the therapy room to be sure he'd really attended. He had, though he hadn't appeared to be doing anything more than watching. That was normal, though. It might take him a few sessions to warm up to the idea, to open up to the other members of the group.

"I know I'm not supposed to talk about what happened in the session, but I have to say, there are some really angry women at this retreat."

"Sadly there are," she agreed. "Anger is the—"

"Second stage of the grieving process," Will recited for her. "I saw the poster."

Will took a bite of his salad, and Abi watched him chew, the way the sharp line of his jaw flexed and his throat contracted when he swallowed. She remembered the way she'd touched his face when they'd kissed. The contrast between the two sides. The uneven, almost velvety surface of his scar and the raspy brush of his beard stubble on the other. It had been so long since she'd touched a man that way—touched a man *at all*. It had made her feel warm and dizzy and excited. Almost feverish.

Not unlike the dreams she'd had last night. They'd been disjointed and hazy but so vivid in passionate detail she'd awoken feeling fidgety and anxious. Even her morning hike hadn't been enough to settle the restlessness.

"You're doing it again," Will said, grinning at her.

She realized she'd completely zoned out, her eyes on his face. *What* was her problem? Why couldn't she stop staring at him?

She lowered her eyes, felt her cheeks color. "Sorry. I don't know why I keep doing that."

"If it were anyone but you, it might bother me." He took another bite of salad, chewing slowly, eyes on her, and she had to fight not to stare back. She took a bite of her sandwich, but the bread felt dry and spongy in her mouth.

"Can I ask you a question?" he said.

She nodded, eyes on her plate. "Sure."

"Why do you always sit alone?"

She didn't usually. She had the first few days of the session only because she'd wanted to keep an eye on Eric and hadn't wanted to be distracted by conversation. And though she would never admit it to Will—it shamed her to admit it to herself—the past two days she'd sat alone in the hopes he would sit with her. Which he had. Both Saturday and Sunday they'd shared lunch together.

"I've been keeping an eye on a few of the kids." A half-truth. She didn't like to lie, not anymore. That was a practice she'd abandoned long ago. But she did have her pride to consider.

"Would you prefer it if I moved to another table?"

"Of course not," she told him, then added, "I enjoy your company."

"Me, too," he said. "And Abi, it's okay if you look at me. I don't mind."

She looked up and saw that he was giving her that infectious lopsided smile. He was adorable and he knew it, darn it, to the point of being a little smug about it, but she couldn't help smiling back.

They ate in silence for a few minutes, then Will said, "Looks like your matchmaking didn't work, huh?"

She followed his eyes to the table where Eric sat alone and all the way across to the opposite side where Leanne shared a table with her father.

"I really thought they might like each other," Abi told Will. "I guess I was wrong."

Will took a swallow of his soda and leaned back in his chair. "Maybe it's better that way, since guests aren't supposed to get involved with other guests."

"They're just kids. They can be friends."

"He's—what?—about sixteen, seventeen? When I was that age, I only thought about one thing."

"Will, she's only fifteen. She's too young for… whatever you're suggesting."

"Don't tell me you've forgotten what it was like when you were that age."

That was something she would never forget, as much as she would like to erase that part of her life from her memory. But what she had been like at that age had nothing to do with what normal teenagers experienced. Will would be appalled if she were to tell him how old she was the first time she'd let a boy talk her into the backseat of a car.

Leanne's parents were getting divorced, but she'd had a relatively normal upbringing. Two parents, an older sibling to look up to.

So different from Abi's life.

"I don't think we have anything to worry about," Abi said. "She's not that kind of kid."

Will shrugged. "If you think so."

She did. She worked with kids all the time. She certainly knew them better than he did and resented his questioning her judgment. He seemed to do that an awful lot.

Honestly she questioned herself enough for the both of them. Maybe that's why it bothered her so much.

"You're angry," he said. "I can tell by the way you're clenching your jaw. You do that when you're upset."

She realized he was right. Her jaw was clenched so tight she was giving herself a headache. She took a deep breath and made an effort to relax the muscles in her face.

"I don't mean to second-guess you. I just have this habit of playing devil's advocate. In my line of work, sometimes it's difficult to see anything but the negative. I'm sorry."

It was funny how those two little words could soften her up. Maybe because she'd heard them so little in her life. Or because she knew that for him the words didn't come easily. When Will said "I'm sorry," she knew he truly meant it.

"You're forgiven," she told him, both hating and loving the way he made her feel. "Besides, if we have to worry about anyone showing inappropriate behavior, it's Leanne's sister, Cindy."

"She has a history?"

She opened her mouth to answer him, then stopped herself. "I shouldn't be talking about this. Sorry."

"It's okay," he said. "I understand."

She glanced at her watch. The under-fives afternoon arts-and-crafts session began in less than ten minutes and she'd promised Adam she would stop in for a few minutes. She rarely passed up the opportunity to spend time with her son. He always came first. "I have to get back to work."

"Will you be eating dinner in the dining room tonight?"

"Most likely."

He flashed her that grin again and she could swear she felt her heart flutter. "Then I'll see you tonight."

She could play devil's advocate, too, she thought as she stood and walked toward the door feeling the weight of Will's gaze on her back. A little voice deep inside was telling her that Will had worked his way under her skin with far too much ease. And despite his faults, of which he admittedly had many, he was just too…perfect. He always seemed to do and say the right thing. And when he made a mistake, he always managed to turn it around and use it to his favor. She couldn't decide if he was incredibly clever or just naturally charming. And she couldn't shake the feeling she was making a mistake.

She seemed to be feeling that an awful lot lately.

Chapter 9

The call Will had been waiting for came Wednesday morning after his group therapy session.

"Ran the names," Robbins said.

"You said Monday or Tuesday," Will barked. He was getting freaking whiplash watching Abi's and his own back—because someone had undoubtedly been following them Monday, Tuesday and again this morning.

But whether that person was following him or Abi, he wasn't sure. Whoever it was had been determined to stay hidden, keeping far enough away so that by the time he was discovered, he had time to disappear before Will could get to him.

"It took some extra time because I had to dig pretty deep," Robbins told him.

"And?"

"And nothing. It was a dead end. Everyone checked out. I found some shady accounting practices and one sexual indiscretion involving an underage prostitute, but no one is linked to the Sardoni family."

Will felt equal parts relief and frustration. Someone *had* been following them. If it wasn't a member of the Sardonis, then who was it? And why?

"You're one hundred percent sure about this?" he asked Robbins.

"Unless there was someone you missed. A member of the staff maybe?"

"I checked. Other than that new guy, Tom, they've all been with the retreat at least a year."

"Will, you should be relieved. Whatever the Sardonis were talking about, it wasn't you."

If he told Robbins what had been happening, that he'd been followed and could possibly be in danger, it was quite possible—probable, in fact—that Robbins would insist on sending another agent in or at the very least contacting the Denver office, and Will's cover would be blown to hell.

He couldn't take that risk.

"I am relieved," Will said. "I just wanted to be sure."

"How's it going? Any closer to meeting the owner?"

"Not yet, but I'm working on it."

"So you, uh, seeing a shrink? That is what they do there, right?"

"Group therapy," Will snapped. "And yes, I'm going."

"Good, if anyone needs it, you do."

Will told him exactly where he could shove his opinion, and Robbins did something he didn't do very often.

He laughed. And before he hung up said, "You know where to find me if you need me."

"Mommy, can I invite Megan to my birthday party?"

"Honey, your birthday is months away," Abi told Adam. "She won't be here then."

His lower lip curled into a pout. "Megan said she had a party with a clown and a pony and a bunch of kids. I want a party like that."

He still had trouble grasping the concept of time and that the kids who visited didn't stay for more than a month. Many for only a week or two. And unfortunately his birthday fell in a month when they hosted an adults-only session. There would be no kids to invite, only retreat staff. Abi couldn't help thinking about what Will had said, about this environment not being stable, about Adam needing friends that lasted for more than a week or a month.

It had been easier when he was younger and didn't form attachments, didn't notice or care that most of his playmates were in their twenties. Now that he was older, he was beginning to realize what he was missing. What would happen in two years when he started kindergarten? The nearest school was almost fifteen miles away. How would she get him there and back with her work schedule? How would he have playdates with friends?

She shook the worries from her mind. She couldn't concern herself with that right now. They would work it out. Everything she did, all the sacrifices she had made, were for Adam. To the point that she never did anything just for her anymore.

Considering the way she'd been feeling lately, the way she'd been questioning herself, she was beginning to wonder if maybe that wasn't such a great thing after all.

"We'll see honey, okay?"

He nodded and walked away, shoulders slumped, and flopped down in front of Maureen's television.

We'll see was becoming her standard answer lately to the relentless requests for things she just couldn't give him. Could he have a daddy or a baby brother or a black puppy with white feet?

Eventually he was going to figure out that *We'll see* really meant *No*.

"What's up with Adam?" Maureen asked, setting two cups of coffee down on the table.

Abi shrugged. "The usual three-year-old stuff. He wants a big birthday party with lots of kids. He just doesn't understand that there won't be any here. It breaks my heart to have to tell him no. I feel like I'm scarring him for life."

Maureen slid into the seat across from her. "Abi, depriving a child of a birthday party is not going to scar him for life. The circuses my mother used to throw for me on my birthday didn't make my life any less dysfunctional."

Abi leaned back and sighed. "It was so much simpler when he was smaller. When he didn't ask so many questions."

"Parenting is not supposed to be easy."

"I know. It just feels like lately I've lost my handle on life." She sipped the steaming coffee and set it back down. "So we've had dinner and dessert, talked about work and my mediocre parenting skills. When are we going to talk about why you really invited me here?"

Maureen smiled. "What gave it away?"

"I've known you long enough to know when something is on your mind."

Maureen paused and sipped her coffee, as if carefully planning her next words.

"Wow, this must really be bad," Abi said, and she had a feeling she knew exactly what Maureen was going to say.

"You know I trust you completely, Abi, and I don't listen to gossip—"

"This is about Will Bishop, isn't it?"

She seemed a bit taken aback by Abi's honesty. "You have been spending a lot of time with him. I don't have to tell you a divorce retreat is not the place to look for eligible men."

"Have you ever known me to get involved with a guest?"

"I don't mean to accuse."

"He's a nice guy and he seems to have taken a liking to me. I've been able to use that to help him." She explained how she'd conned Will into attending the therapy sessions.

"Abi, I'm your friend as well as your boss. As your

friend, I'm going to tell you to be careful. The man is here for a reason. I'd hate to see you get yourself into a situation where you're setting yourself up to be hurt. Take it from the queen of poor judgment. If you're going to have a relationship with a man, try to find one with as few issues as possible."

They'd both made their share of bad choices where the opposite sex was concerned. "I know that."

"As your boss, I need to ask you, no matter what may come of this, to use discretion."

"Or?" ·

"That's not a threat, Abi. I just can't have the other staff thinking this is acceptable behavior."

"I understand."

She was cutting Abi a lot of slack. Anyone else would have been placed on probation, and had the behavior continued, their employment would have been terminated.

"You're sure you know what you're doing?" Maureen asked.

She wasn't sure about much of anything this week. Last session if this had become an issue, Abi wouldn't have hesitated to put an end to whatever behavior was bothering Maureen.

Last session she'd hadn't known Will.

Since Abi and Adam were locked up tight in Maureen's fortress, Will had a few hours off from playing bodyguard. To pass the time he hung out in the game room, where he could keep an eye on the stairs that led to Maureen's apartment on the second floor. He had a drink with Larry and shot a few rounds of pool, then went outside to the patio by the pool—knowing Abi would have to pass it on her way home—stretched out in a lounge chair and watched, beer in hand, as the sun inched its way toward the horizon.

He may not have bought into the therapy garbage they were selling here, but he couldn't deny he felt relaxed for the first time in he didn't know how many years. He was actually enjoying the time away from work, out of the field. He'd always loved his job, loved being an agent, but lately it felt as if the only thing keeping him going was the need to get Collucci behind bars.

Robbins had been urging him for months to take a week or two off. Maybe Will just needed a little recoup time and the passion for his work would return. Maybe then he would feel like his old self again.

In his peripheral vision Will saw the door to the main building open, and Abi stepped out with Adam slumped in her arms. He was considering how he would approach her without her knowing he had been waiting for her when he realized she was walking in his direction.

As she approached, he looked up at her and smiled. "Hey."

"Hey."

She didn't say anything else, just stood there looking uneasy.

He sat up and set his empty beer bottle on the table beside him. "What's up?"

She looked in the direction of her cabin, then back to Will. "Could you walk with me to my cabin?"

Here he'd been trying to find an excuse to do just that, and she'd saved him the trouble. "Yeah, sure."

"I have to get this kid in bed," she said. "He weighs a ton." She shifted him from one hip to the other, and Will realized he was out cold.

"I'll carry him," Will said without thinking. Not that there was any reason he shouldn't, he'd just never thought about carrying someone's sleeping kid.

Abi looked wary. "Are you sure? He's heavier than he looks."

He held out his arms. "I don't mind at all."

Abi shrugged and handed him over, and Will "oofed" as all that dead weight landed in his arms. "I told you he's heavy," she said.

Will gathered the boy's lanky little body to his chest, and Adam's eyes fluttered open. He looked sleepily at Will, smiled, then wrapped his arms around Will's neck, dropped his head on his shoulder and was out again.

Will and Abi started in the direction of the employee cabins. Will had the feeling something was up, but she was silent. When they reached the path that led to her porch he asked, "So are you going to tell me what's up?"

"Let's get him into bed first."

They walked up the steps together and she unlocked the door, holding it open for him. "You can just lay him in bed."

In Adam's room she pulled back the covers on the bed and Will laid him down. Adam curled in a ball on his side and Abi covered him with the sheet. They walked silently out of the room.

"Would you like a beer?" Abi asked.

"Do I need one?"

She grinned and he felt some of her tension ease. "It couldn't hurt."

She got two beers for them, then gestured to the couch. She sat in the corner and he sat facing her, his arm draped along the back.

She took a long pull from her bottle, then turned to him and said, "I had a talk with Maureen tonight."

"About?"

"You."

Uh-oh. He took a swig of beer and set the bottle on the coffee table.

"I guess there's been talk. About us spending so much time together. I can't say I'm surprised."

"Are you in trouble?" He truly believed she needed someone keeping an eye on her, but he didn't want to be the one responsible for getting her fired.

"Not exactly. She just…she's worried about me. And how it will look to the other employees."

"I thought we had decided we were just going to be friends."

"Yes, but it might not look that way to other people."

"That's not our fault."

"No, it's not, and it's not fair, but it's just the way things are. If I were any other employee, Maureen would have all the excuse she needed to put me on probation. She won't because we're good friends, but I feel wrong taking advantage of that."

"So what are you saying?"

She paused, took another swig of her beer, and he waited for the worst, for her to say that they couldn't even be friends.

He wasn't even sure if he could accept that. And not only because he felt she needed his protection but because of the way he felt about her. He really enjoyed the time he spent with her, the time with her son.

She was right. It wasn't fair that they had to worry about what other people thought, what conclusions they might draw.

"I was going to tell you we shouldn't see each other anymore. Even as friends." She stopped, bit her lip.

"But?" He hoped there was a "but" there. That this wasn't some sort of brush-off.

"Since Adam was born, my entire life has revolved around taking care of him," she said. "Every decision I've made was for his welfare, whether I thought it was good for me or not. Now all I seem to do is second-guess myself."

"That's probably my fault."

"No, it isn't. All you've done is make me stop and take a look at things, really see my life. Lately I've been feeling like…like I'm disappearing, I guess. As if the only identity I have is being his mom. I'm afraid that eventually I might grow to resent that. That's not fair to me and it's not fair to him.

"I spent the better part of my adult life being self-ish and the last four completely selfless. I have to find a middle ground." She turned to him, her knee bumping his shin, and slid a hand over top of his on the back of the couch. "Maybe it's not smart and a little selfish, but I don't want to stop seeing you, Will. I want us to be friends."

He hadn't realized until then that he was holding his breath. He exhaled slowly, feeling dizzy with relief.

"If that's what you want, too," she added, looking a little uncertain.

"It is," he assured her, and she smiled. He reached up and brushed back the lock of hair that had fallen across her face, tucking it behind her ear. How could he have ever thought she was plain? There was a beauty there, a radiance, that shined from the inside out.

And the thought of her being hurt, of him not being able to protect her and her son, burned a hole in his gut the size of a baseball. He lifted the hand resting over his and laced his fingers through hers.

"We should try to be more discreet," she said. "Maybe not spend so much time together in front of the guests and staff."

"If we have to avoid being seen together when other people are around, let me go hiking with you tomorrow morning," he said. That way he would get to spend time with her *and* keep her safe. It was a win-win situation.

"We had an agreement."

"I'll keep going to the therapy, I promise." It wasn't really all that terrible, so continuing to go wouldn't be that big of a hardship. And just maybe he would learn something. "I want to spend time with you."

"I don't know…."

"I know you have a hard time trusting, Abi, but give me this chance. I swear I won't let you down."

She thought about it for a minute, then smiled. "Meet me at the trail behind the main building tomorrow morning at six-thirty."

Chapter 10

Will glanced up at the clock above the door in the therapy room. Fifteen more minutes and he could get back to looking after Abi. Though he knew she was probably safe with all the kids around, it made him uneasy not being able to keep an eye on her.

Saturday therapy wasn't technically part of the deal, but Abi had given in and let him hike with her Thursday and Friday despite their original agreement, and it seemed to mean a lot to her that he go. Considering the sacrifices she was making for him—like testing the boundaries of her friendship with Maureen to spend time with him—he kind of felt as if he owed her. He didn't like the idea of owing anyone anything—in fact, it was something he avoided—but with Abi he didn't mind so much. It didn't feel like a burden. It was more like…well, the truth was, he didn't know what to think of the way he felt about her. It wasn't about sex—not that he didn't think about getting her into bed.

Constantly.

It went beyond that, beyond what he'd felt for his wives. Something complicated yet effortless, exhilarating but peaceful. He was—

"Will?" Eve said. "Are you still with us?"

He looked around and realized everyone was staring at him.

"Yeah, sorry," Will said.

She turned to Larry and asked, "So what is it that you have in common with these younger women?"

Back to the age thing again? Somehow the discussion always seemed to sway in that direction.

"We do a pretty good job of sweating up the sheets," Larry cackled.

Claire shot him an evil look. "You're disgusting."

"No, Claire," Eve said. "Larry has a valid point. He and the women he marries are sexually compatible. That's very important in a new relationship. The newness and the excitement of learning each other. But that doesn't last forever. Not to say that you can't continue to have a good sex life. But eventually something else takes its place. Does anyone know what that is?"

Will looked around the room, but no one seemed to know what she was talking about.

"Friendship and respect," Eve finally said. "Did you consider any of your wives a friend, Larry?"

Larry shrugged. "I don't know. I guess I never really thought about it."

Friendship and respect.

Will considered what Eve was saying and realized he'd never really thought about it, either. And as corny as it sounded, even to him, something in his brain clicked—like the flipping of a light switch.

Had he been friends with either of his wives? Had he respected them?

He shifted restlessly in his chair.

Eve turned to him. "You look disturbed, Will. Is there something you'd like to say?"

"No, I just…" He shook his head. "Never mind."

"No, please tell us."

"It's nothing."

"Tell me then, what's your definition of marriage?"

"Definition?"

"Describe your relationships with your wives."

He shrugged. "I don't know. You meet, you date for a while, you get married."

"Then what?"

He shrugged. "What do you mean? Then you're married."

"What happens then? You live happily ever after?"

He laughed. "Hardly. For a couple of months it's fun. The sex is good and it's nice to have someone to come home to at night. A hot meal waiting on the table. But then they start to complain incessantly and…*cling*. You can't go out for a beer without a lecture and they nag you until your fillings ache. You find yourself working longer hours just to get away. You shut off your phone because they call you fifteen times a day and you're tired of hearing them whine. Tired of hearing that you're too closed off emotionally or you don't love them enough. And when you can't take it anymore, you leave."

When no one spoke, he gazed around and discovered that everyone was staring at him in stunned silence.

"Wow," Larry said. "That's harsh."

"Do you feel you're *not* closed off emotionally?" Eve asked.

He thought about it for a second and realized he probably was. "No. I am."

"Why do you think that is?" Eve asked.

It was his father. No matter how hard Will tried to be different, it always came back to that. "I'm a lot like my old man, I suppose."

"Your parents were divorced?"

"No, they were married for thirty-five years. But they weren't good years. I don't think they were ever what you could call happy."

"That's an interesting observation," Eve said. "Let me ask you all this. How many of your parents had what you would consider good marriages? Raise your hands."

Everyone looked around, but no one raised their hand. Hell, wasn't *anyone* happy? What was the point of getting married if it only made you miserable?

"How many had parents who divorced?"

Five of the eight raised their hands.

"So," Eve said, "it's possible that your failed marriages could in part be due to learned behavior."

"Meaning what?" Jade asked.

"As children, we learn by example," Eve said. "When our only example of marriage is one of dysfunction, doesn't it make sense that we ourselves might have troubled marriages?"

"So what?" Roger asked. "Anyone who was raised in a broken home is cursed to have a failed marriage?"

"Of course not. But statistics don't lie. There is a higher probability that a child raised in a split family will as an adult have marital problems, as well."

Was that Will's problem? Had his parents' dysfunctional relationship warped him somehow?

"Sounds like a major cop-out," Roger said. "Blaming our parents for our own mistakes. Where's the accountability?"

"Of course we can't blame everything on our parents. But family relationships, as well as outside influences, can have a lasting effect on a child's psychological development. And of course the opposite is true, as well. Children from happy families might also end up the victims of divorce."

"So basically what you're saying is we're all screwed," Jade said.

Eve smiled. "All I'm saying is that there is no one cause or reason that people behave the way they do. But by being here and talking things through, maybe we'll begin to recognize what it is that has gone wrong in our own relationships and learn what to do to change that behavior." She looked at her watch. "Time to wrap it up people. I'll see you all Monday morning."

For the first time since starting therapy Monday he

was sorry it was over. And for the first time he had something to say, had questions.

Could it really be that simple? His marriages hadn't worked because he hadn't seen his wives as friends? Hadn't respected them? He could see now that his marriages had been about toleration. About sticking it out until they drove him so completely out of his mind with frustration he'd had no choice but to leave.

"Are you okay, Will?"

He looked up and saw that Eve was standing by the door and the rest of the group had left already.

"I just…" He shook his head. "It's just something you said."

She walked back over. "Something that upset you?"

"Sort of, I guess."

"It's okay to talk about it, Will. That's why I'm here."

He looked up at the clock. "It's time for lunch—"

"We can be a little late." She sat down across from him. "Tell me what's bothering you."

"I kind of feel like…like someone punched me in the head."

Eve smiled. "Why is that?"

"It's just that whole thing about a husband and wife being friends. It makes sense. I guess I just never thought about it. Now I'm wondering why. Why didn't I see it before?"

"Your parents weren't friends?"

"Hell, no. I don't think they even liked each other. Looking back, I'm not sure I liked my wives much, either. Maybe at first, but later…" He shrugged. "Later I just felt suffocated. That sounds awful, doesn't it?"

Eve leaned forward, hands clasped. "You mentioned your wives were clingy. Something about that trait must have attracted you to them."

"I suppose at first the attention was okay."

"They made you feel special?"

He nodded. "You could say that."

"Did your parents make you feel special?"

He lifted an eyebrow at her. "We're back to blaming my parents?"

"Humor me."

He sighed and sat back, giving it some thought. "No, I guess they didn't make me feel special."

"Did you feel loved?"

"Not particularly."

"Think about that for a minute. How did that differ from the way you felt with your wives?"

He thought about it and he actually had a pretty good idea of what she was suggesting. And even more, it kind of made sense. Maybe there was something to this therapy stuff. "What you're saying is I was attracted to them even though they were overbearing and clingy because they filled some sort of emotional hole left by my parents."

"You felt needed. Everyone likes to feel needed."

"But they got so demanding and dependent, eventually I just felt smothered."

"And maybe you resented them for not being stronger?"

"I did. It used to drive me crazy that they couldn't seem to make a move without consulting me first. I hated it."

"But they weren't the ones who changed."

"No," he agreed. "It was me. I'm the one who changed."

"Well," Eve said, rising to her feet. "I've given you plenty to think about. I'll see you Monday morning."

"Yeah. See you Monday."

So he'd been right all along. He was the one who'd screwed up his marriages. He was the one with the hang-ups.

But what good was that knowledge if he didn't know how to use it? And how could it stop him from making the same mistake again?

Abi watched Will from the opposite side of the bonfire. Something was definitely up with him. It was rare to see him without a smile on his face, not engaged in conversation. Tonight he kept to himself and he looked...troubled.

He glanced up at her and grinned—and yes, caught her staring again—and she got that giddy, excited sensation in her stomach.

A smile like that from a man had never stirred these schoolgirl-crush feelings. Years ago, after her mother had left her, it used to mean a place to sleep for a night or a week. A nice meal out instead of cheap fast food or a sandwich at the shelter. Later, when she'd realized the full extent of her effect on the opposite sex and how to use it, it might have meant a gold necklace or a diamond bracelet she could later hock when the goodwill and interest dried up.

Now she resented her mother more than ever for not

teaching her how wrong that was. She hated her for showing Abi that cheating and lying and using were just ways to get by.

But that was in the past. She was a different person now. She only hoped that when the truth came out, when she told Will what she used to be like, it wouldn't change the way he felt about her. Even if she wasn't sure exactly how he felt now.

One by one the guests and staff went back to their cabins. Only a few stragglers remained when Will finally sat on the log beside her, stretching those long, lean legs in front of him. His forearm brushed hers and little shocks of awareness zapped through her. Maybe it was due to the fact that they had been avoiding each other the past couple of days, trying to keep up the illusion that they weren't becoming inappropriately involved.

She tried to look casual, keeping her eyes fixed on the smoldering logs, watching spirals of smoke drifting up into the star-filled sky.

Eric walked up to them, hands in his pockets.

"Do you need anything else, Abi?"

Abi smiled up at him. "I don't think so, Eric. Thank you for all your help tonight."

"Sure." Eric shot Will a curious, almost suspicious look and hesitated, as if he wasn't sure if he should leave the two of them alone.

"You can head back to your cabin now," she told him.

He hesitated a second more, then ambled off into the darkness, toward the visitor cabins.

The last two guests called good-night and headed off, as well, leaving her and Will alone.

For several minutes they sat there quietly watching the remnants of the fire pop and crackle and burn themselves out. They weren't doing anything improper, but she couldn't help feeling the slightest bit naughty.

"You've been quiet tonight," she said. "Is everything okay?"

He looked over at her and smiled. "It is now."

A wash of warm tingles swept over her again. What was it about being with Will that made her feel so good?

A cool breeze rolled across the lake, and she rubbed her bare arms.

"It's getting cold," Will said. "And late. Can I walk you back your cabin?"

"I'd like that."

He stood and held out a hand to give her a boost up. It was such a casual gesture, she didn't think twice about taking it. His hand was warm and a little rough as it curled around her own, and suddenly she wasn't cold anymore. That excited feeling in her stomach began to corkscrew slowly outward.

Instead of letting go, Will laced his fingers through hers. She considered pulling away, but it looked as though everyone had either retired for the night or, considering the level of noise, gone to the bar or games room in the main building. No one would see them, so what harm could it cause?

By the light of the stars she let Will lead her in the direction of the staff cabins. She used to think it was so quiet here compared to the noisy chaos of the cities she'd grown up in. But that was only because she hadn't been listening. All around them a symphony of sounds filled the night air. The calming lap of the water over the sand. The melodic chirp of crickets hiding in the forest floor. The hum of the wind and the rustle of leaves that lay in its path.

Now that she'd made a home surrounding herself with nature, there was no going back. She could never live in the city again.

They followed the path leading into the woods under a dense canopy of foliage, blackness folding over them like a cool velvet shroud. Up ahead she could see the dim glow of her porch light.

Home.

She'd never really had one before. She'd lived places—if you could call the way she used to exist *living*—but this cabin among the trees was where she'd felt at peace for the first time in her life.

Somewhere off to the left of where they walked Abi heard the crunch of a twig snapping, and Will's grip on her hand tightened.

"It's probably just a stray animal," she said. "We get a lot of raccoons at night."

"It doesn't bother you?" he asked. "Being so isolated? So far from civilization?"

"Not at all." From the isolation she drew a deep sense of security she'd never once felt in the city. "You live in the city?"

"Manhattan for the past couple of years. When I was married, I had a place in Jersey. I don't miss the commute."

"You like it there?"

"I like the convenience of being able to walk around the corner for a six-pack. I don't plan to stay there forever, though. It would be a nice change to be out of the city, away from the suburbs. Maybe after I retire."

They neared her cabin and their pace slowed, as if neither wanted the evening to end. They'd pretty much waited all day for this time together. She wanted it to last.

"What will you do then?"

"When I retire?" he asked and she nodded. He paused for a moment, then laughed lightly. "It's probably going to sound ridiculous...."

"Tell me."

"I want to be a writer."

"Why would I think that's ridiculous?"

"A lot of people would."

"That's only because they don't know you."

He looked down at her through the dark. "And you do?"

"I know that you're not the kind of man to give up. Or the kind not to do something because someone told you not to or thought you shouldn't."

He chuckled. "Yeah, I guess you're right." He gave her hand a gentle squeeze. "You know, you're the first person I ever told that to."

"You didn't even tell your wives?"

"Nope."

"How come?"

He shrugged, tugging lightly on her arm. "I guess because they never asked."

He sounded so…sad.

"What's wrong, Will?"

He shrugged again. "I've just had things on my mind."

"Anything you want to talk about?"

"Not really. I don't mean to be emotionally distant. It's just something I need to figure out on my own."

She couldn't help smiling. "Emotionally distant?"

He laughed. "Hey, you're the one who talked me into the therapy. Now you have to deal with my psychobabble."

"It's good to know you've been paying attention. Maybe you don't think it was such a waste after all?"

"You know I don't like admitting I'm wrong, but in this case, you were right. The therapy has been…enlightening."

That made her happier than she'd expected it to. She'd done what she had set out to do—she'd helped him. She couldn't ask for more than that.

But she wanted more, she realized. She just wasn't sure what.

"I'm glad to hear that. Just so you know, I'm always here if you need to talk."

He gave her hand another squeeze and asked, "What about you? Do you always want to be a counselor?"

"When Adam is in school I'd like to go to college. I'll have to go part-time, probably nights, meaning I'll be at least forty by the time I get a degree. But it's something I've always wanted to do."

"Why is that?"

"To prove to myself that I can. My mother bailed

when I was seventeen and I had to support myself, so I didn't finish high school. I never had much in the way of skills." Not the marketable kind anyway.

They stopped a few yards from the door, far enough away from the light, so that anyone looking would see only shadowy forms. "Thank you for walking me home. I'd invite you in, but Brit is here. I know what she would think."

Through the dark she could see that lopsided smile. "It's late. I understand."

She wished she could ask him in. She wished they could sit and talk for hours. Maybe because when she talked, he really listened. She'd never had deep, meaningful conversations with men. The kind of men she'd dated hadn't been interested in conversation. They'd wanted arm dressing and a good time in bed. They used to treat her as if she had an empty skull under all her teased hair, when nothing could be further from the truth. And she'd used that misconception to her advantage, to get what she wanted.

If she'd had a different upbringing, the right opportunities, she might have gone far. She still could, she told herself.

"I guess I'll see you around tomorrow?" he said. "Maybe we could have lunch together."

"Tomorrow is my day off. Sometimes I leave the retreat."

"Okay then, Monday morning for a hike?"

She heard disappointment in his voice and couldn't deny feeling the same emotion. She wished they could have spent more time together this evening, but it was so late. And Monday was an entire day away.

Did she really want to wait until then to see him again?

"What are you doing tomorrow?" she heard herself ask.

"Golf maybe. I hadn't made any definite plans," Will said. "Why do you ask?"

"I planned on taking Adam into town. I promised him. If you aren't busy, I thought maybe, if you wanted to—"

"That sounds like fun," he said.

"I mean, we don't do anything special. We just look at the shops and get ice cream and there's a park where we sometimes stop and have a picnic—"

"I said yes, Abi. I'd love to spend the day with you and Adam." He reached up to cup her cheek with his free hand. "As long as you're not worried about people seeing us together."

It was so difficult to think straight when he touched her that way. She wondered if he knew it. "I suppose it's possible we could run into someone there. But we wouldn't be doing anything wrong. Right?"

"Of course not." His fingers slipped over her skin, and that warm place in her belly began to simmer again. Then he slowly lowered his head.

He was going to kiss her right there in front of her cabin.

Instead of pulling away, her breath caught and her eyes drifted closed. She felt the heat of his breath on her face, caught the scent of smoke from the bonfire on his skin. Her knees felt weak and her head a little dizzy.

She knew it was wrong to do this, but she wanted it anyway.

Her lips tingled and her heart pulsed in her chest. She lifted her chin, anticipating the feel of his mouth against hers. Instead he brushed a kiss very lightly against her cheek.

She nearly groaned with disappointment. After anticipating a kiss, yearning for it, she wanted to feel it.

His lips lingered for several seconds and then he slowly backed away. Acting on pure instinct, she wrapped her hand around the nape of his neck, pulled him down and pressed her lips to his.

There was a second of surprise, of hesitation, before his body relaxed and he leaned into the kiss. He teased her lips with his tongue, coaxing her to open up. His mouth was soft and warm and persuasive. She'd kissed a lot of men, but she didn't think she'd ever met anyone who did it quite this well.

And a kiss wasn't enough this time. She wanted more. She wasn't even sure what she wanted, only that she ached for it. For some sort of…connection.

She pulled her hand loose from his and wound her arms around his shoulders. Her breasts crushed against his chest, tingling as they pulled into tight, aching points. Their thighs brushed, knees bumped. Bare skin touched bare skin. The sensation was so unexpected, so erotic, her insides melted into liquid heat.

This is what it's supposed to feel like, she realized. This was real passion. This was lust.

A spark of something bigger, something deeper, ignited her blood. How could she have gone her whole life and never experienced this? This absolute connection with the opposite sex?

Because sex hadn't been about connection. It had been about control and manipulation—survival.

She felt herself moving, felt him easing her backward, until she collided with the unrelenting surface of a tree. Through her shirt she felt the rough bark cut into her skin, but instead of discomfort she felt excitement. She was pinned in place, trapped by the weight of his body, but she didn't feel confined or afraid, she felt…liberated. She wanted to be taken, *possessed*. She wanted to know what it felt like to let go, to be out of control.

Her hands wandered across the width of his shoulders, down the lean muscle of his chest, curling into fists around the fabric of his T-shirt. Will groaned and his arms tightened around her, pulling her more firmly against him. His hands were in her hair, on her face, touching, exploring.

The kiss became more urgent, and she felt herself sinking deeper, spinning out of control. So carried away she nearly forgot where they were.

Any of the staff could walk by and see them. This had to stop now—before they *couldn't* stop.

She broke the kiss, feeling breathless and dizzy. "I probably shouldn't have done that."

He pressed his forehead to hers, eyes closed, sounding out of breath himself. "You won't hear me complaining."

Though she knew they should part, she couldn't make herself move. "What are we doing, Will? We both know this can't happen."

"Can't or shouldn't? Because it can, I think we just established that."

She couldn't hold back a smile. He was right. In the sexual-attraction department, they were batting a thousand. "We shouldn't because it's against the rules. I can't because I have a son to think about, a good life here that I can't risk throwing away. There's too much at stake."

He took a long, deep breath and blew it out, tousling the hair by her ear. "How about what you *want?*"

That was the problem—she didn't know what she wanted. Two weeks ago everything had been clear. Life had been simple and easy. Then Will had come along and her world was suddenly chaos.

"Forget about me, Will. What do *you* want?"

Chapter 11

What *did* he want?

Hell, he wasn't even sure anymore. Things he'd never imagined he'd want again. Things he'd thought were out of his reach, like marriage and family. Companionship. When he was with Abi, it felt possible. Complicated and confusing and frightening as hell—but possible.

The strange part was, he liked her too much, cared too deeply to subject her to life with a man like him. At least, not until he got his head together. He might know where he went wrong with his past relationships, but that didn't mean it wouldn't happen again. She deserved better. And she was right—there was so much to consider. More than even she realized.

Eventually he would have to tell her the truth, tell

her why he was really here. Though he hadn't directly lied to her, he hadn't been completely honest either and he knew how important trust was to her. She could easily interpret his omission as a betrayal.

And then there was Adam. He was a great kid—smart and funny and creative. And desperate for a father figure, if the way he'd latched onto Will was any indication. But what kind of role model would he be? He knew nothing about raising a child.

Well, that wasn't entirely true. He knew the wrong way—his father had taught him that.

"Why don't we take this one day at a time?" he told Abi. "We won't make any promises or have any expectations, not until we *both* know what we want."

She nodded, looked relieved even. "Okay."

"It's late. I should go."

She nodded again and he backed away. He wanted to kiss her again, to touch her, but he knew if they got started, they may not be able to stop and things would probably go further than either of them was ready for.

Did he want to sleep with her? Hell, yes. But not if it meant hurting her or Adam.

"Are we still on for tomorrow?" he asked.

"If you still want to come."

"I do."

"Then meet us in the main parking lot at ten."

"I'll be there."

She hesitated, looking up at him through the dark. For a second he thought she might kiss him, but then she turned and walked to her cabin. When she'd stepped inside and closed the door behind her, he headed down the path. Somewhere beside him he heard the rustle of underbrush, and his hand automatically settled into the pocket where he kept his switchblade. He strained to see into the woods, but it was too dark. He couldn't see three feet in front of his face.

Unfortunately Abi was wrong—it wasn't a stray animal. Someone had been watching them.

He just had to figure out who and why.

Abi leaned back on the blanket they'd spread out in the grass near the playground in Laurel Valley City Park.

She tipped up her head, letting the early-afternoon sunshine warm her face, the quiet breeze ruffle her hair. She closed her eyes and breathed in the sweet scent of honeysuckle, listened to the sounds of children playing, the squeak of the swings and the thud of little feet against the wood play equipment.

It was so…peaceful.

Four years ago, before Adam, she would have never appreciated the simple pleasure of spending an afternoon on a blanket in a park. And she wouldn't have appreciated the easy companionship of the man stretched out on the blanket with her.

Will lay on his side next to Adam, head propped up in one hand as they both examined some green, spindly, creepy-looking insect that had landed on their blanket. The two were so close their heads were nearly touching. To anyone observing, he could have easily been mistaken for Adam's father. And she couldn't stop the emotion from building in her when she looked at the two of them that way.

She realized now that her hopes of Adam not getting attached to Will were futile. Superglue couldn't increase the strength of the bond that had developed between the two of them. And how could she expect Adam not to grow attached when she herself had slipped so deeply under Will's spell?

It was almost embarrassing the way she'd lain awake half the night wondering what it would be like to spend the day with him. The way her stomach had jumped with nerves and excitement as he'd walked toward them in the parking lot that morning. The way she could so easily forget what was right, abandon common sense for that emotional connection, the physical pleasure of being near him. The idea of touching him, the memory of the kiss they had shared last night, the way his body had felt pressed against her, made her feel intoxicated with desire, heavy with lust. Even though lust was the last thing she should be feeling in the middle of a busy park.

Maybe later, when they got back to the retreat, she would invite him in for a while. Then, when Adam went to bed...

They would what? Kiss? Touch? Would she invite him into her bedroom? It felt too soon for that, yet the idea filled her with curiosity. Was that her idea of waiting until they knew what they wanted—taking him to bed?

That was the old Abi. She didn't want to be that person anymore.

Beside her Adam reached up and placed a small, sticky hand on Will's cheek. "Will, is your face ever gonna look normal?"

"Adam!" Abi scolded. "That's not a nice thing to say."

"It's okay," Will said and told Adam, "It's a scar. It won't ever go away."

Adam considered that for a second. At three, the concept of time, of forever, was often lost on him. "You got burned?"

"That's right."

Adam's eyes widened. "By acid?"

"Adam," Abi said in a stern voice. "You know it was a fire. I've told you a dozen times."

Will grinned and chucked him under the chin. "Burned by acid is more exciting though, isn't it, sport?"

Adam nodded enthusiastically, his dark head bobbing up and down.

Most men would have been exasperated by the endless questions Adam asked, uncomfortable with his insatiable need for attention. Will was so patient and understanding.

So…natural.

That didn't mean he would be anything more than a good babysitter. It took more than that to be a father. Not that he was auditioning for the role or anything. Which made it that much more special. He wasn't trying to impress her. He was just being himself.

She gave herself a mental shake. She shouldn't even be thinking about things like that. They were nowhere near that point in their relationship—might never be. And after his visit at the retreat was over, they may never see each other again.

Adam stared intently at Will's face. "Did it hurt a lot?"

"It sure did."

"More than a bee sting?"

"Probably more like a thousand bee stings," he said and Adam's eyes went wide. "That's why you should never play with matches or fire. It's very dangerous."

Adam poked him lightly in the cheek. "Does it hurt?"

"No. It gets itchy sometimes, though."

"When a 'squito bites me and it gets itchy, mommy puts the pink stuff on. Maybe she could put it on your face."

"Pink's not exactly my color, but I appreciate the offer." Will grinned and ruffled Adam's hair. There was so much affection in the gesture, Abi felt tears push to the surface. She thought for sure she was going to lose it right there in the park. He probably had no idea what it meant to Adam, what it meant to her.

"Mommy, can I play in the sand?"

She swallowed and said, "Sure, honey. Just be careful."

Adam grabbed the action figure Will had bought him at the local toy store, hopped up and darted in the direction of the sand and play equipment, where half a dozen other kids played. When Abi turned back to Will, he was gazing off in the direction of the trees bordering the north end of the park, eyes searching, as if he were looking for something…or some*one*.

"Anything wrong?" she asked.

He turned back to her, and she saw that Adam's

hand had left a smudge of ice cream and dirt on his cheek. "Huh? No, nothing is wrong. Just…thinking."

She grabbed her backpack and rifled through it for a wet wipe. She found a pack under her pepper spray, pulled one free and held it out for him to take. "Adam got dirt on your face," she said.

Instead of taking the wipe, he tipped his cheek toward her and asked, "Could you get it?"

She didn't know why, but the idea of touching his face, even if it was only to wipe it clean, felt so…intimate. And he knew it, she could tell by the look in his eyes. He was testing her.

She leaned over and gently dabbed at his cheek.

He closed his eyes and sighed. "Feels nice."

She lingered there, several seconds after she'd wiped the last of it away, then tucked the soiled cloth in the front pocket of her pack. "I thought you couldn't feel much on that side."

"I could feel that." He looked up at her, desire swimming in the depths of his eyes. "Even when I'm not touching you, I can still feel you, Abi. Do you know what I mean?"

She nodded. She knew exactly what he meant. It was an aura of sexual energy that crackled between them whenever they were close.

His eyes searched her face, a long, lazy exploration that made her feel naked, stripped bare emotionally. Finally he zeroed in on her mouth. She knew what he wanted even before he said it.

"I would really like to kiss you right now. Even though I know I shouldn't."

"I would, too," she admitted, feeling warm with desire, as if she were drowning in estrogen. His mouth was inches away. It would be so easy to lean forward and press her lips to his. But Adam might see and become even more confused. And it wasn't unusual for guests or staff to visit the city on free days. Being here together looked suspicious enough. A kiss would start a gossip frenzy.

Will folded a hand around hers, rubbing the inside of her wrist with his thumb, setting fire to her insides. Men had touched her more intimately, more scandalously than she cared to remember or admit, but no one had turned her on as thoroughly as Will did. Much more of this and she was afraid she would melt.

"The truth is, I'd like to do more than kiss you," he said. At the look in his eyes—as if she was the most desirable woman on the planet—she almost did melt right there on the blanket into a quivering puddle of female hormones.

Men had desired her, that was nothing new. But she didn't think they'd ever really seen her, seen past the teased hair and tight clothing to the real woman inside. She'd never let them. Or maybe Will was the only one who'd looked hard enough.

"So would I," she said and his hand tightened around hers.

"What you do to me..." He shook his head, looking as perplexed by this as she was. "I've never felt this way about a woman. I know that sounds like a line—a really lousy one—but I don't know how else to say it."

"I know what you mean. I don't understand it, either."

"It wasn't like this with Adam's dad?"

He almost sounded jealous and it made her smile.

"No. My relationship with Adam's dad was one of…convenience."

"You weren't married?"

"No. He wasn't the settling-down type. We wanted very different things from life."

"You said he wouldn't have been much of a father."

"He would have tried. He would have loved Adam and taken care of him, but sometimes that isn't enough." She hugged her legs and rested her chin on her knees. She didn't even like to think what her life would be like if she were still with Adam's father. Didn't want to remember that phase in her life at all. Some things were better left alone. "There are people who just aren't meant to be parents."

"So you're saying it's better that Adam didn't know him? I'm not being judgmental," he added quickly. "Just curious."

She knew what it was like to grow up without a father, to be the only one in her class without a mommy *and* a daddy, to fake a stomachache on bring-your-daddy-to-school day so the other kids wouldn't look at her and whisper. It was horrible and lonely, but a bad father could be far worse than no father at all.

"I'm saying that I believe everything happens for a reason. I was probably better off not knowing my father, either."

"You've never tried to find him?"

Hard to find someone who didn't have a name. "I was the product of too much tequila and a one-night stand in a cheap hotel. Mama didn't get a name. She was only seventeen."

"You have an accent," Will said, sounding surprised.

She made a face. That happened sometimes when she got caught up in the past and she hated it. It made her sound too much like her old self, the one she wanted to forget. "Yeah. We lived in the South for a while when I was growing up. It sneaks through every now and then."

"It's cute. It fits you somehow."

Absolutely nothing about the way she used to be was cute. And she was letting this conversation ruin what so far had been the best day she'd had in a very long time. "How about your parents? What are they like?"

"My father was a drill sergeant. My mom was a housewife. He spent most of their marriage ordering her around. She spent it doing what he asked."

"Did you get along with him?"

"Every over-the-top, hard-assed cliché you've seen on television of a drill sergeant—that was my dad. He didn't *get along* with anyone."

By Will's harsh tone, it was clear there was a great deal of animosity there. She could relate.

"No siblings?" she asked.

"Nope. Could we possibly change the subject? Talking about family puts me in a rotten mood."

Well, they had that much in common.

He curled a hand around her ankle, stroking it with

his thumb, and flashed a sexy, crooked smile. "Can we go back to talking about kissing instead?"

A shadow fell over them as someone walked up and a familiar voice said, "My, my, this is cozy."

Will let go of Abi's ankle and sat up. He recognized the girl from the retreat. Cindy somebody. From the first time he'd seen her he'd had the feeling she was a problem teen, and Abi had confirmed that. She wore her bad attitude like a badge of honor. He didn't doubt she was there to cause trouble.

Behind her, looking uncomfortable, stood the new retreat counselor. The one who *wasn't* a member of the Sardoni family. Will wondered if they had been the ones he'd seen lurking through the woods bordering the park.

"What can I do for you, Cindy?" Abi gazed up at the girl, looking more than a little annoyed. Then she saw Tom standing behind her and the look went from annoyed to peeved. "Hello, Tom."

"Hey, Abi." He shifted uncomfortably, as if he knew he'd screwed up.

Cindy crossed her arms over her chest. "Hmm, I wonder what the other staff would think if they knew you were here playing touchy-feely with a guest."

Will sensed trouble and made a move to get up, but Abi rose to her feet first. Despite being shorter than both Cindy and Tom, in attitude alone she towered over them.

Whoa.

He'd been all prepared to come to her rescue, but she clearly didn't need rescuing.

"Where is your father, Cindy?" Abi looked ready to bite their heads off, but her voice was dead calm, intimidatingly so. She was usually so friendly and patient with the kids. It looked as if maybe her patience had finally run out, at least where Cindy was concerned.

"He's probably at the retreat playing golf," Cindy said. Her words had bite, but her wary expression said she realized she'd pushed too far.

"Does he know you're here?"

The girl glanced away and shrugged.

Abi's expression darkened. "Is that a yes or a no?"

Double whoa. If the kid knew what was good for her, she'd give up the tough act.

"Even if he did, he wouldn't care," Cindy snapped.

Abi turned to Tom, barely contained anger hovering just below the surface, and the kid went pale with fear. "I'm sure I don't need to tell you how inappropriate it is that you've brought a minor guest here without her father's permission."

"Whoa, Abi, I didn't bring her here. I was here and we ran into each other."

"How did you get here, Cindy?"

Cindy flashed her a defiant look and held up a thumb. Will shook his head. The kid apparently had no clue how dangerous it was to hitchhike, especially in such a remote area. Or maybe she didn't care. Maybe it was some sort of ploy to get her father's attention. One that could have easily gotten her raped or murdered and dumped in a ditch.

"Mr. Bishop and I are going to take you back," Abi said.

Looked as though their pleasant afternoon was over. Will stood and started folding the blanket.

"What makes you think you can boss me around?" Cindy said. "You're not my mother."

"Tom," Abi said, "would you please go fetch Adam for me? He's playing in the sand."

Tom looked relieved to be given a free pass out of this mess. "Sure, Abi."

"Aren't you the hypocrite," Cindy said in that tone kids used when they were trying to raise themselves to an adult level. If she thought she could intimidate Abi, she'd been mistaken. Abi didn't flinch.

Damn. Every time Will was sure he had her pegged, she would reveal some new facet to her personality.

She grabbed the blanket from him, stuffed it into her backpack and said, "Let's go."

Cindy threw her shoulders back and lifted her chin in one last fruitless effort to shift the balance of power. "I don't want to go back, and you can't make me."

Abi gave her a look that would have put Will's father in his place and said calmly, *"Watch me."*

Chapter 12

"Five more minutes until bedtime," Abi warned Adam, who was playing with his toy trucks in a dirt patch beside the cabin. She and Will sat side by side on the swing on her front porch, nursing bottled beer, quietly enjoying the evening.

When they'd returned from town that afternoon, Will had intended to invite himself over for dinner, but Abi had saved him the trouble and extended an invitation—right in front of Cindy, proving yet again she was not a woman to be messed with.

Rather than hang around and witness the fireworks that were sure to ignite when Abi handed Cindy over to her father—not that he wouldn't like to see the kid get what was coming to her—he'd gone to his cabin and called Robbins to see if there was anything new

from the wiretaps. There wasn't, and Will said nothing about the individual who'd been following them.

Now that he was back there with Abi, he was wondering if they might, as Cindy had so succinctly put it,
get to play touchy-feely again.

This wasn't like him at all. He had a job to do here,
but somehow that kept getting pushed aside. In the
past he'd always been one hundred percent focused.
Especially times like now, when he was so close to
solving a case. But for the first time in four years his
quest for justice had been overshadowed by a much
more basic need, something Will had never felt before.

Emotional connection. The need to be Abi's friend
as well as her lover.

His wives had been physically beautiful, but in the
end, pathetically lacking in most other departments.
Abi was the whole package—beautiful and desirable
on the inside and out. And the more he got to know her,
the more time he wanted to spend with her, the further
ahead he began to look in terms of what kind of future
they might have together—and what his life would be
like if, after the remaining two weeks were up, they
parted.

Two weeks. Damn, he could barely believe it had
only been fourteen days since he'd first lain eyes on her
in the office. Of course, he had a reputation for rush-
ing into relationships. He'd married his first wife after
three months, his second after five. It was probably the
newness of it, that euphoria of feeling *needed*.

Being with Abi had felt like that, too, almost from
the moment he'd met her. And maybe at first it had

been that desire to be needed that had drawn him to her, but since then, especially today, she'd made it pretty clear she didn't *need* him for anything.

Maybe what he found most fascinating was that she always had him wondering what new thing he would learn about her.

"I'm sorry I ruined our afternoon," Abi said.

Will swirled the beer in the bottom of the bottle. "You didn't ruin anything. In fact, it was highly entertaining watching you lay into Cindy. The kid needed to be put in her place."

"I know she's troubled and confused, but she made me so angry. I probably shouldn't have been so hard on her."

"No, you were perfect. I guarantee she'll think twice before messing with you again."

"She might say things about us being together at the park, and I wouldn't put it past her to embellish."

"So what do you want to do?"

"There's not much we can do."

"We could stop seeing each other." Just saying the words left a painful hole in his gut, and he wished he could take them back. What if she agreed? He didn't *want* to stop seeing her.

"That would be the responsible thing to do," she agreed and he felt it like a sucker punch. He never should have opened his big mouth.

"The thing is," she continued, "I'm really tired of always doing the responsible thing. I'm sick of planning my every move, of worrying about what's going to happen and how I'll deal with it. So let's *not* do the responsible thing, okay? Just this once."

That didn't mean they shouldn't be smart. "How irresponsible are we talking here?"

"I'm not saying we shouldn't still be discreet."

"So no skinny-dipping in the lake?"

She gave him an exasperated look. "It's so nice to
know you're taking me seriously."

He grinned and took a swig of his beer.

Boy, he really liked her.

"I can't stop people from thinking what they want
to think," she said.

"Does this mean that when no one else is around we
get to stop pretending we're only friends?"

"If we're going to be honest with each other and with
ourselves, it seems like that's the only thing we can do."

"I'm all for honesty." Though too much of it could
be a bad thing at this point. "What about Adam? How
do you want to handle that?"

She took a deep pull on her beer, draining the bottle.
"With caution and discretion until we know for sure
where this is going. As you've probably noticed, he's
grown very attached to you. I don't want to see him get
hurt."

"I don't, either."

"Speaking of Adam…" She glanced at her watch
and called, "Time to go inside, kiddo."

"Aw, man," Adam whined. "Do I *gotta?*"

"You *have to*," she corrected. "It's past nine. You'll
have to skip your bath and hop right into bed."

He walked to the porch, shoulders slumped, tennis
shoes dragging, and then he saw Will sitting there and
brightened instantly. "Can Will tuck me in?"

She looked over at Will and he nodded. "Yes, Will can tuck you in."

Adam darted up the steps and grabbed Will's hand, pulling him up out of his seat. "Come *on!*"

"One book," she called after them, but there was a catch in her voice. Will looked back at her as Adam dragged him into the cabin and through the fading light of dusk he could swear he saw tears shimmering in her eyes.

Will finished the book Adam had picked out from the loaded shelves on his bedroom wall and set it on the table beside his bed. It was about a family spending a day at the park.

"I don't have a daddy," Adam said. He sat beside Will in his pajamas, his head resting on Will's arm. "I just have a mommy."

"Your mom told me."

"Can I call you Daddy, Will?"

Wow, that was unexpected. "Why would you want to call me Daddy, sport?"

"I want a baby brother, but mommy says you can't have a baby without a daddy. If I call you Daddy, then maybe she'll have a baby."

Will suppressed a grin. Not bad reasoning for a three-year-old. He could swear sometimes he felt as if he was falling as hard for Adam as he was for his mother. "I'm not sure if calling me Daddy would be such a good idea. It might upset your mom."

His bottom lip curled into a pout and his shoulders drooped. "Okay."

"Besides, it takes a little more than that to have a baby. For starters, the mommy and daddy should be married." At least, that's the way *he* thought it should be done.

"Can't you and mommy get married?"

"To get married, you have to love each other."

He looked confused. "You don't love my mommy?"

Oh, man, stick the knife in and twist it a few times, kid. "I like your mommy a lot, but I just met her. It takes time to learn to love somebody."

"You never learned how?"

He wasn't quite sure how to answer that. Sure, he'd felt love, but not the kind a man should feel when he makes the decision to commit to someone for the rest of his life. So he answered honestly. "No, I think I'm still learning."

Adam looked up at Will with pleading eyes. "One more story?"

Amazing how quickly the kid could change gears. "Not tonight. Your mom said just one."

He got up and Adam snuggled down under the light covers.

"Could you read to me again tomorrow?"

"Maybe." If he was here, he wouldn't mind reading to him, but that was Abi's call. He didn't want to make a promise he couldn't keep.

He tucked the blanket around Adam and switched off the lamp, hesitated a second, then pressed a kiss to his forehead. "See you tomorrow, sport."

His eyes were drifting closed and his voice sounded sleepy. "Night, Will."

Will stepped out of the room, heart in his throat, and shut the door quietly behind him. He didn't know exactly why he'd kissed Adam good-night. It had just felt like the right thing to do. Maybe it was wrong. He just didn't know anymore.

Everything felt all confused and jumbled up. He didn't know *what* he wanted.

He walked into the family room to look for Abi. The room was lit by a single dim lamp beside the couch where she lay sleeping.

She looked like an angel lying there, and he couldn't help but wonder if he had any idea what the hell he thought he was doing. If just by being here he was putting her and her son in danger. He hoped that by now whoever was following them had figured out Abi wasn't the one they were looking for. They must have or they would have made a move by now. He wished he could tell her the truth, who he really was, and trust her not to tip Maureen off. But even he knew that was too much to ask.

As deeply as he cared for Abi, he had an obligation to Ryan's family. They needed closure, and so did he. He had to see this through.

He walked over to the couch and as he sat on the edge of the cushion, she roused, looking up at him through sleepy eyes.

"Adam?" she asked.

"He's asleep."

"Oh, good." She yawned and stretched her arms over her head. "I guess I dozed off."

"You're tired," he said, brushing a lock of hair back from her face. "I should go."

"I don't want you to go. Not yet." She slipped her arms around his neck and smiled up at him. "This is me not pretending we're just friends."

He had the feeling he was really going to like this honesty business. He lowered his head to brush his lips over her forehead. "What did you have in mind?"

"I'd like to take you into my bedroom, but I'm not sure if I'm ready for that."

"To be honest, I'm not sure if I am, either. Not that I don't want to, believe me. I just think, all things considered, it would be better if we took this slow." He wasn't sure where this was going and he didn't want to get in too far over his head before he told Abi the truth.

Abi wound her fingers into the hair at his nape. "We could kiss for a while."

"If Adam woke up, he would see us and there would be questions." He thought about telling her the entire "Daddy" business, then decided against it.

"He wouldn't see us if we turn the light out."

"And if he wakes up and finds us in the dark?"

She reached over her head and switched off the lamp, plunging them into darkness. "We'll tell him we're playing hide-and-seek. He'll buy that."

Before he could object, Abi pulled his head down and kissed him—hot, sweet and demanding, as if she knew exactly what she wanted and wasn't afraid to take it. It was the exact opposite of what he'd expected, and desire slammed him hard and fast.

"Lie down with me," she murmured and scooted to give him room.

He stretched out beside her, looked down at her through the dark. "Are you sure about this?"

"I'm not sure about anything anymore. But it's what I want."

Will kissed her in that slow, hypnotizing, mind-numbing way he was so good at, and Abi felt herself melting again. And though she knew it was probably wrong, she didn't care. All she cared about, all she knew, was the need to be close to him. The rest they would figure out later.

He caressed her face, touched her hair, her shoulder, the dip just below her collarbone—places she'd never considered particularly arousing. But with Will doing the touching, a warm, restless ache began to build between her thighs. In the past she'd been more or less numb when it came to the region below her waist. Of course she'd felt things, but they hadn't been particularly exciting or even pleasurable. Sex was just something she did to keep a man happy, to bend him to her will. She hadn't known it was supposed to feel like this.

He cupped her breast and she groaned softly.

"Is this okay?" he whispered against her lips.

"Yes." It was so much better than *okay*.

He caressed her through her shirt, one breast, then the other. Men had always been particularly drawn to them, but she couldn't remember one ever touching her so tenderly.

The ache burned hotter, spread to her stomach and breasts. Then his hand slipped under her shirt, touched bare skin, and she gasped in a breath.

Will froze. "Not good?"

"No," she said, "it's very good. Don't stop."

His hand slid upward, over her stomach, up each of her ribs, until he was touching her through the lace of her bra. All the while he sipped at her lips, kissed her chin and her throat, nibbled her ear. Drove her crazy.

This gentle, lazy exploration was so different from the way she'd been touched before. Most men expected satisfaction and they would take whatever they wanted to get it. They'd never cared much if it was enjoyable for her. Or maybe she just hadn't let them try.

Satisfying her was *all* Will seemed to care about. Not that he objected when she slipped her hands under his shirt and ran a palm up his lean, muscled torso. He made a noise, somewhere between a moan and a sigh, and kissed her more deeply. She'd imagined touching him this way so many times. Fantasy paled in comparison to the real thing.

Will eased her shirt up, the cup of her bra down, and cool air tickled her. Then he was touching her—his warm palm against her oversensitized bare skin. If she wasn't trying so hard to be quiet, she would have moaned.

"You're beautiful," he said, watching her body react as he touched her, his voice rough with desire.

Lots of men had told her that, but they had only been words. She didn't think a single one of them had looked at her, seen her the way Will did. She wasn't very big on top, and nowhere close to her pre-pregnancy firmness, but he didn't seem to mind. His body, on the other hand, showed few signs of age. Everywhere her hands wandered she encountered only lean, well-toned muscle, firm skin. Even the hair on his chest felt silky-fine.

"My body was better before I had Adam," she said.

"No. You're perfect just the way you are."

He lowered his head, touched her with his tongue. The sensation was so shockingly intense, a deep shudder quaked through her and she dug her nails into his skin. He teased lightly—one side, then the other. The ache between her legs, the wet heat, became unbearable. She *needed* him to touch her, needed release from this torture. But somehow she didn't think he would make the first move.

Oh, what the heck.

At the risk of being too much like the old Abi, she grabbed his wrist and guided Will's hand down over the front of her shorts.

Chapter 13

Will's head snapped up in surprise. Playful petting he'd anticipated, but nothing this intimate. At least, not yet. Not that he didn't want to. There was nothing more exciting to him than pleasing a woman.

He loved every scent and flavor, every contour and texture of the female body. He might have been a lousy husband in many respects, but in the bedroom he'd never heard a single complaint. Good sex was probably the only thing that had held his marriages together in those final taxing months. But he didn't want Abi to feel pushed into something she wasn't ready for.

He looked down at her hand clutching his wrist, then up at Abi's face. He was going to ask if she was sure, if it wasn't too soon, but then he saw the look of tortured ecstasy in her eyes. Her cheeks were flushed bright red, her lids half-closed.

There was no question she new exactly what she wanted. And God knows he wanted it, too.

He fumbled with the button on her shorts, but his fingers felt rubbery and uncoordinated. The reality of them lying here together like this really had him in a state. Almost twenty-five years of sexual experience under his belt and he felt like a damned kid again. He was actually nervous, the way he'd been in tenth grade when he'd touched a girl this way for the first time on the couch in her parents' den—so scared they would be caught by her father but too turned on, too curious, to stop.

Maybe he was nervous because he knew how important this was, what it meant to her to take this next step. He didn't want to do something wrong and screw this up.

Abi reached down and yanked the button free.

He was only a little embarrassed that he was coming across as so inept. "Thanks."

"No problem," she said, her voice breathy and deep.

Will lowered her zipper, and she sighed—long and slow and deep. He slipped his hand inside the opening, over top her panties, and she hissed out a breath, eased her legs apart. Through the silky fabric he could feel how wet she was, how ready to be touched, but he wasn't about to rush this along. He was going to savor every second.

Abi reached down and tugged at the button on his shorts.

He pulled his hand free and grabbed her wrist, the way she'd done to him. "You don't have to."

"I know I don't," she said. "That's why I want to. That's what makes it so special."

His heart stilled in his chest. What did she mean by that? Was she trying to say she'd been forced to do things against her will? "Abi, are you saying that you were…"

He couldn't even make himself say the word.

"I wasn't raped, if that's what you're thinking. I've just done a lot of things for the wrong reasons. This feels right." She smiled up at him. "Now where were we? Oh, I remember…."

Her eyes locked on his. She shook his hand from her wrist, took hold of it and guided him back down to the opening of her shorts. He slipped his hand inside, this time going directly inside her panties, watching her face. As his fingers brushed her warm, slippery folds, she moaned and her eyes rolled up, her thighs easing farther apart.

He was wound so tight already, so turned on, he knew he wasn't bound to last very long, but he let her unfasten his shorts. He didn't stop her when she lowered his zipper. His breath hitched and his muscles tensed as her fingers brushed his stomach. He kept up his tender stroking, not missing a beat when she slipped her hand under the elastic waist of his boxers and gripped him gently. He sucked in a breath and his free hand fisted in her hair.

She rubbed her thumb back and forth across the tip, over the slippery moisture there. Will groaned and muttered a curse, feeling the familiar tightening in his groin already starting. At this rate, it would be over in about ten seconds.

Then, by some miracle, she stopped.

"Take your shirt off," she demanded. And he could see where Adam got his bossiness from.

"But, Adam—"

"He won't wake up."

"Abi—"

"Please. I want to feel you against me." She pulled her own shirt over her head and peeled her bra off without bothering to unhook it. It would seem she wasn't self-conscious about her body after all. He wondered if anything he'd thought about her that first day was true anymore. And if not, well, that was okay, too.

He raised up on one elbow and yanked his shirt up over his head, then dropped it on the floor behind him where it would be convenient to grab if Abi was wrong and Adam did wake up.

They lay down facing each other, her breasts warm and soft against his chest, their legs intertwined, and didn't waste any time picking up where they'd left off. They slowly caressed and stroked each other, eyes locked. This wasn't just two people making each other feel good. This was absolute intimacy and closeness, total trust.

But it wasn't long before need and instinct took over, actions became bolder and breath quickened.

"Kiss me, Will," she whispered.

Their lips barely brushed when she moaned and began to tremble all over. Feminine muscles contracted and gripped his fingers. He was so close, teetering right on the edge, ready to fall over. Then she reached down with her other hand, touched him just below the family jewels, and he lost it. He smothered a groan against her lips as every part of him clenched and locked, then let go in a rush of absolute pleasure.

They rode it out together, wave after wave of erotic sensation, then just held each other.

For some stupid reason Abi felt like crying. With Will's arms wrapped around her, their bodies touching, she felt so safe, so…complete.

She'd vowed a long, long time ago never to need a man to make her feel like a whole person, but this wasn't something she could control. It was just there, in her heart. Touching each other this way, sharing something so personal, had done something to her, changed her somehow, and she knew somewhere deep in her soul she could never go back.

"Abi?"

Abi looked up to find Brittney hovering over her desk and wondered how long she'd been standing there. Big surprise, she'd been daydreaming about Will again, about what they had done Sunday night. For three days it was all she'd been able to think about. That and what they would do when they met at her cabin tonight. Since Sunday they'd barely had a minute together, much less any intimate time. Monday night Adam had a combination of too much sun, too much candy and too much fun and was up late with a tummy ache. Early Tuesday morning Abi had left for an overnight camping expedition on the other side of the lake with the ten-and-older kids and hadn't gotten back until this afternoon.

Tonight nothing was going to stop them from being together.

"Hello? Earth to Abi."

Abi gave her head a shake. "I'm sorry, Brit. What did you want?"

"I came in to ask if you'd talked to Tom like you promised."

"Talked to Tom?" she asked, drawing a total blank.

"About him screwing around, not doing his work. Abi, we discussed this over a week ago!"

Damn, she'd completely forgotten. "Yeah, of course."

"So did you?"

"I'm sorry, Brit. I guess I've been a little preoccupied. I'll talk to him today, okay?"

"I can't take this anymore, Abi. It's like he doesn't know *anything* about being a camp counselor. I have to tell him how to do everything. Even then, he either doesn't do it or he does it wrong."

"Maybe he's just used to doing things a little differently."

"That's not it."

"He has excellent references."

"I don't care what his references say," she snapped. "If he doesn't get his act together or you don't fire him, I swear to God I'll quit."

"Whoa, Brittney, hold on—"

"You know he's screwing around with the guests. He takes that girl to his cabin."

"That's a strong accusation to make." One she hated even to consider, since she was guilty of the same thing. Tom knew the rules. It was likely another employee she'd seen going into his cabin and not a guest.

Or this could be Brit's wounded pride talking.

"I understand that you're upset. Sometimes when we feel rejected, we get hurt and we lash out."

"Rejected?" She looked confused, then her cheeks went pink. "You think I *like* him?"

"You don't have to be embarrassed—"

"Even if I did—which I don't—at least he's not a *guest*," she challenged.

Abi didn't have to ask what she'd meant by that or deny that she deserved it.

"And I don't listen to gossip or draw any conclusions until I have all the facts," Abi said.

Brittney dropped her eyes to the floor. Abi could tell she'd made her feel bad, which of course filled her with guilt.

"I will talk to him today," she said gently. "I promise."

Brittney nodded, then walked out.

It wasn't like the girl to be so judgmental and she loved her job. She would never quit without a very good reason. Abi had to consider that Tom really was causing a problem. And maybe his being in town with Cindy Sunday hadn't been an accident after all. Maybe Cindy had claimed to hitchhike there to protect him.

Abi would have to get to the bottom of this.

Her phone rang and she answered it.

"Abi," Susie said. "We have a problem in the therapy room. Some kind of fight between two of the kids. Eve wants you to come there right away."

"I'll be there in two minutes."

She hung up the phone. As if she didn't have enough on her plate already. Looked as if that talk with Tom would just have to wait.

"They were leaving the afternoon therapy when it started," Eve told Abi. "I caught them fighting next to the building."

Abi stood beside her in the therapy room, trying to figure out the best way to deal with this mess. Leanne sat on one side of the room in a chair beside her father. He had an arm protectively around her and was glaring across the room at his older daughter, Cindy.

Tearstains streaked Leanne's cheeks and one side was scratched and bleeding. One of her eyes was swollen and turning blue. On her part, Cindy had the beginnings of a fat lip forming on the left side of her mouth. Their clothes were filthy, as if they'd been rolling in the dirt, and their hair was in shambles.

This was no sisterly spat. Someone had been out for blood.

"Either of you want to tell me what happened?" Abi asked.

"That's what I'd like to know," their father said, shooting Cindy an accusing look. "What did you do to your sister?"

"Oh, so you automatically assume this is my fault?" Cindy spat. "How typical. You *always* side with her."

Leanne looked up at her father, tears brimming in her eyes. "I don't know why she hates me so much."

"First hitchhiking, now beating up your sister?" her father said. "Why are you doing this?"

Cindy shot her sister a dirty look. "Why don't you ask *her?* She started it."

"I'm asking *you.*"

"No matter what I say, it's going to be my fault, so what difference does it make?"

"I'm going to have to talk to Maureen about this," Abi told their father. "Any physical altercation between guests is grounds for immediate expulsion from the program without a refund. Since the fight was between sisters and no one else was hurt, she might be willing to cut you some slack."

"Dan, why don't you take Leanne to the nurse and have her scratches cleaned and her eye looked at?" Eve told their father. "I'll have a talk with Cindy."

He nodded and stood, then said to Cindy, "Until we straighten this out, you are on house arrest, young lady, understand? You can go to meals and therapy, but that's it."

Cindy shot him and her sister a look of pure hatred as they stood and walked out the door.

"I'm going to go talk to Maureen," Abi told Eve and added quietly, "See what you can get from Cindy."

"So," Maureen asked after Abi had explained the Cindy/Leanne situation, "how do you think we should handle this?"

Like Abi, she was more sad than angry. Sad that

after more than two weeks of therapy Cindy was no less angry or confused than when she'd arrived.

"I think we should let their father deal with them."

"According to the rules, which are very clear on the matter, they should be expelled from the program."

"There are extenuating circumstances."

"Are there? Or are you losing your objectivity?"

She knew exactly what Maureen was alluding to. Abi had asked herself that same question a dozen times on her way to her office. If she cut them a break, would people think her own behavior was a motivator? Or if she stuck to the rules, would people see her as a hypocrite?

All she could do was try to keep her personal feelings out of it and make a decision based on the facts.

"Since no one else was hurt and they are sisters, I think they should be given another chance. Their behavior is a clear indicator that they could benefit from further therapy."

"And you're prepared to deal with any backlash you may get from the other staff over your decision?"

She understood where Maureen was coming from, but she couldn't help feeling angry—at herself as much as at Maureen. For four years she'd been a faithful employee, had done everything by the book, with no regard for her personal life aside from her son. She shouldn't be made to feel guilty for finally taking something for herself. Yet she couldn't blame anyone for judging her. No matter how much she cared for Will, she was still breaking the rules.

This was getting so complicated.

"If you want me to stop seeing him, say it," she told Maureen.

"Would you?"

The question stopped her.

The truth is, she didn't know. Was he worth losing her job over if she were given an ultimatum? How could she risk that when neither she nor Will was sure yet where this was going? She couldn't be so irresponsible, not with her son to think about. But Will would be gone in ten days. Could she pass up the opportunity to get to know him, to be with a man who, for the first time in her life, she'd even come close to falling in love with? A man who might someday be a father to her son? Would *that* be fair?

"No," she told Maureen. "I don't think I would."

Maureen leaned forward. "And you should know me well enough to realize I would never ask you to make a decision like that. Not when in a week and a half he'll no longer be a guest here. And I think you're right. There are extenuating circumstances in the fight this afternoon. They should be allowed to stay."

"If you agreed with me, why the third degree?"

"I wanted to be sure you were confident in your decision." She smiled. "And I believe that you are."

"I'll let the girls and their father know."

"I can't force you to make a decision about Will, Abi, but I also can't shield you from what the staff may do or say."

"I realize I'm in no position to expect any more special treatment. I can deal with the staff."

"Good." She sat back in her chair and folded her

hands on her desk. "Can I ask you a question? As a friend?"

"Of course."

"Do you love him?"

"I...I don't know. I'm not sure if I even know what that is. He's so unlike any man I've ever known. I like the way I feel when I'm with him. The way I feel about myself and the way he makes me feel. I...I *trust* him."

"Does he feel the same way?"

"I think so."

"What about Adam? Does Will want to be a father?"

"I think he might. He's so good with Adam, and Adam adores him."

"You've only known him two and a half weeks. He lives in New York, you live in Colorado. What will you do? A long-distance relationship? Will you leave the retreat?"

"I don't know yet. We just know that we want to give this time to develop. I know we're going to have to talk about it soon. With work and taking care of Adam, there just hasn't been time. I have no evening activities tonight, so we were planning on having dinner together. I suppose it's time I bring it up."

"Maybe I could take Adam. Give you two some alone time to figure this out."

"I hate to ask you—"

"You didn't ask. I offered. Bring him by around five. He can spend the night."

"Oh. That's not necessary. Our relationship hasn't... I mean, we haven't—"

"It'll give as much or as little time as you want."

Maureen gave her a smile. "You deserve to be happy, Abi. I hope this works out."

"I know that if you met him, you would love him."

"Then why don't you bring him to dinner?"

"Really? You're sure?"

"If you trust him, then I do, too. And If I'm going to give you my blessing, I have to get to know the man, right?"

"When?"

"How about tomorrow night? Say six o'clock?"

"I'm sure it will be fine. I'd better go have a talk with Cindy's father. Let him know they're staying. And thanks, Maureen, for being so understanding about everything."

Maureen gave her a smile and turned back to her computer screen.

Abi left Maureen's office wondering what she would say to Will, how she would ask him what he wanted. She didn't want to rush things or put him on the spot, but with only ten days left they were going to have to start talking about where this was going and what their expectations were. Did he want a committed relationship? And if so, how did he feel about her son? Adam didn't need a stepdad, he needed a father, someone who could love him like his own.

And if she discovered they were on a completely different page in terms of the future, she would have to end it now. Tonight. Before she let herself fall too hard and was in too deep. The last thing she wanted was a broken heart.

Though she couldn't help wondering if she was in too deep already.

Chapter 14

"Bishop is getting in to see her tomorrow night," Mikey told Vince.

"You're sure."

"I heard 'em talkin' today. It's definitely tomorrow."

Vince's heart pounded, his blood pulsing with the lust for revenge. "We've gotta handle this very carefully. We can't let her get away again and we can't let the FBI get to her first. She can't testify."

"If it's her, he's going to want her on the first plane outta here."

If the feds got her first, Vince would never get his money—if there was any left. "I have to take her first. Before the feds have time to get there."

"You?"

Mikey was family and loyal to the death, but this

time Vince couldn't afford any mistakes. If it was Crystal, he was going to be there when it went down. To see the look on her face when she realized she'd been found. The fear in her eyes when he told her exactly what he planned to do to her. And he wanted to be there to get his money. "I'm catching the next flight out. I want you on them every second. The minute you know anything, you call me and I'll meet you at the retreat."

"What about Bishop?"

"No witnesses, Mikey."

"He's an agent."

"Wouldn't be my first."

"What if it ain't her? What then?"

It was. He could feel it. Besides, Bishop had been looking over his shoulder for four years. He was tired of it. Maybe it was time to send a message to the FBI. "I'll kill him anyway."

He was finally getting in to see Maureen.

Abi had told him that afternoon when they'd passed each other on the beach—she'd been on her way there with a group of kids, and he'd been on his way back from a swim. It had taken every bit of self-restraint Will could muster to keep his response passive when Abi had told him the good news.

He would know tomorrow night if Maureen was Crystal. And if she was, he would have his witness and Vince would finally go down.

He should have been bouncing off the walls with adrenaline and instead he was wracked with indecision.

And he knew exactly why. There was no doubt in

his mind he was falling in love with Abi. The more he went to therapy, learned what made him act the way he'd acted, the more he believed that they had a shot together. That he could be a good husband and maybe even a good father. He realized he wanted the chance to try. But there was the very real possibility that when she found out why he was here, it could be over. She might never forgive him for not being truthful, for turning in her friend. She may not understand why this was so important to him. And he couldn't blame her if she didn't.

So could he give it all up for her? Could he call Robbins and tell him the trip had been another dead end and finish out his time here as a guest, Abi never being the wiser? Could he let Vince go free? Could he break the vow he'd made to Ryan's wife and children—to himself—and still face himself in the mirror every morning?

The answer was no, he couldn't.

He had to finish this. No matter the consequences. If this relationship with Abi was meant to be, she would understand. He would find a way to make her understand. After he met Maureen. If he told Abi now, she might tip off Maureen and she'd be gone. He might never find her again.

"So you told their father that they can stay," he asked Abi after she told him about the situation with Leanne and Cindy that afternoon. They were just finishing up the dinner dishes.

"Yeah. From what Eve was able to get from Cindy, there's a guest her sister likes. I'm guessing it's prob-

ably Eric. Leanne saw Cindy with him and got jealous.
Cindy swears Leanne started the fight."

"Do you believe her?"

"I'm not sure. If it's true, I can understand why
Leanne is upset. Cindy knew from the start that Leanne
liked him. She's so mean to Leanne all the time. Maybe
she just snapped. It doesn't mean it's okay to attack her
sister. And I'd hate to see Cindy blamed for something
she didn't start."

"Is there anything you can do?"

"Not really. It's up to her dad to sort this out. I can
only hope he'll be fair."

He set the last of the clean silverware in the drawer
and hung the damp dish towel over the oven handle to
dry. Abi was rinsing the sink, so he stepped up behind
her and slipped his arms around her waist. He loved
touching her, being close to her. The scent of her skin,
the softness of her body.

When he'd first met her, he'd seen her as being more
like his wives in personality. Quiet, reserved, maybe a
touch self-conscious. He couldn't have been more
wrong. He wished he could pin down the thing that intrigued him, solve the mystery of why she appealed to
him. But maybe some mysteries weren't supposed to
be solved. Maybe there was no clear answer. Things
just were what they were.

She sighed and rested her head back against his
shoulder. God, it felt so good to hold her. Just to be with
her. It had been a long couple of days waiting for some
time alone together. A long, uncomfortable night hiding in the woods, keeping an eye on her camping

group. He would be so happy when this was over, when Vince was behind bars and he could get on with his life.

He was already tossing ideas around about what he would do when this trip was over. It was possible he could get a transfer out to this part of the country. It would be a slower pace, low-profile cases. In fact, he'd heard field offices in cities like Denver could be downright stagnant. But he would be close to Abi and Adam. For once he could put work on the back burner and focus on his personal life, maybe even write a chapter or two in his spare time. Have a couple of kids.

A future that felt hazy and unclear two weeks ago was suddenly coming into focus. It could happen—if he didn't blow it.

"What would you like to do now?" Abi asked.

He flattened his hands over the soft swell of her belly, pulled her close so she could feel just how nuts she made him. "What would you like to do?"

She made a soft purring noise in her throat and turned in his arms, sliding her hands up his chest and around his neck. "How about this?"

She got up on her tiptoes and brushed her lips over his, sinking her fingers into his hair.

Kissing was good.

Then she abruptly stopped and dropped to the balls of her feet. "Oh, crap."

"What's wrong?"

"I just remembered, I was supposed to have a talk with one of the employees today."

"You were kissing me and thinking about work?"

She grinned. "I'm sorry, it just popped into my head. There was a situation I promised I would handle."

"It can't wait until tomorrow?"

She looked up at him apologetically. "I'll just stop by his cabin really quickly. It should only take a few minutes. I promise."

Will sighed and dropped his arms from around her. "I'll walk with you."

"Oh, you don't have to."

"I know, but it's getting dark. I don't like you being out alone at night."

She gave him that look—the one that said she thought he was being ridiculous. "Will, this is not the city. Besides, it's only two minutes away."

"Humor me. I promise I won't interfere."

She shrugged. "If it means that much to you."

They stepped outside together and she closed the door behind her.

He raised an eyebrow at her. "You're not going to lock that?"

"Even if there was a thief here, there's hardly anything worth stealing in there," she said, starting down the steps.

Except maybe his sidearm in his backpack sitting on the floor beside the couch. He'd been keeping it with him whenever possible since someone had begun following them. Whoever it was appeared to have backed off, but that didn't mean their shadow was gone for good. Maybe he or she was just being more careful.

"Besides, we're only going to be gone a minute." She folded her arms across her chest and gazed up at him. He could see that arguing the point wasn't going to get him very far. She'd already compromised by letting him come along and now she had that *look*. That look that said I've made my decision and you're not going to change my mind.

"Are you coming or not?"

When he didn't move, she shrugged and headed down the path toward the other, smaller cabins.

She sure could be stubborn.

Maybe that's why he liked her so much, admired her even. She knew what she wanted and she wasn't afraid to go after it.

Hell, his backpack was on the side of the couch. Even if someone did sneak in, odds were they wouldn't see it. He took the steps two at a time and caught up with her. "So who are we going to see?"

"Tom Sterling," Abi told him. She could kick herself for forgetting about this earlier. She'd been so preoccupied with the situation that had occurred between Cindy and Leanne, talking to Tom had completely slipped her mind. But she couldn't go back on her promise to Brit. She owed her.

And she couldn't wait to get it over with so she and Will could get back to her cabin and their evening alone. She'd decided that they would have a little fun first, then talk about the future. That way, if they decided this relationship should end, she would have at least had one last chance to kiss him and touch him again.

It was completely selfish, and she was just setting herself up to be hurt, but she didn't care. It was what she wanted.

They walked side by side. Hints of dusk peeked through the trees, but around them the forest was dark and quiet. Peaceful. Tom's cabin was the farthest from hers to the east. Warm light glowed through the curtains and the inside door was open.

"I'll just be a minute," she told Will when they reached the porch. He hung back as she climbed up.

She lifted a hand and rapped on the screen door. Though she could see that the bed was unmade and there were dirty clothes and towels strewn everywhere.

"Come in!" he called, she was guessing from the bathroom, since she didn't see him in the room. "I'll be right out."

She stepped inside, kicking a pair of discarded tennis shoes out of her way. His duffel bag was sitting open on the floor half-full, as if he were prepared to make a quick escape.

That was her past talking. In Tom's case, it could simply be that he was too lazy to unpack—which was very possible since he was obviously too lazy to clean, either.

The bathroom door swung open a second later and steam billowed out, followed by Tom.

Wearing nothing but a smile.

Oh, boy.

When he saw it was her standing there, he froze and the smile slid from his face. For a few long seconds neither moved. They just stood there staring at each other.

"Tom," she finally said, breaking the spell, keeping her eyes pinned to his face. "My, this is awkward."

"A-Abi." He frantically reached behind him for a

towel and covered his…equipment. Not that she was looking at it.

Well, she might have taken a quick peek.

"I—I thought you were someone else," he said.

"Sorry. I'm very sorry. I wanted to have a talk with you, but it looks like this might not be a good time."

He glanced nervously behind her through the door, then back to her face. "Uh, yeah, not really."

"If it makes you feel any better, it's nothing I haven't seen before. I mean, obviously I haven't seen your particular—never mind."

He was looking at her as if she was a loon.

"How about we talk tomorrow morning in my office? Seven-fifty?"

He nodded and clutched the towel. "Yeah, okay. Seven-fifty."

"I am very sorry," she added.

"It's okay. I should have asked who it was."

"I'll see you tomorrow." She turned and slipped out the door. Will was still waiting for her at the bottom of the steps. She hooked her arm through his and dragged him toward the path. "Let's go."

"That *was* quick."

"I'm going to talk to him tomorrow."

He looked back toward the cabin. "Why not now?"

"He was…busy."

"Busy doing what?"

"Showering."

"He was in the shower?"

"Well, no. Just getting out, actually."

"He wasn't…." He trailed off.

"Naked? Yes, he was."

His steps slowed. "How naked?"

"There are no degrees to nakedness, Will. You either are or you aren't."

He stopped altogether and she turned to face him. It was pretty dark, but she could see he was frowning. "What I mean is, he was wearing a towel, right?"

"Nope, no towel."

"He was *naked?*"

"Isn't that what I just said?"

"What did you do?"

"We just sort of stood there looking shocked, I guess."

"Did you cover your eyes?"

"Um…no." Honestly the thought had never occurred to her.

"Why not?" he said, sounding indignant. "Does he always answer the door naked?"

He was jealous. How incredibly sweet.

"How should I know? He thought I was someone else. He's expecting company. Which is why I'm talking to him tomorrow." She wondered which lucky member of the staff he was entertaining, then had a disturbing thought. What if it wasn't one of the staff? Suppose Brit was right, and he was messing around with a guest. He'd seemed awfully anxious to get rid of her. Cindy's father had said she was on house arrest, but what if she'd snuck out?

Up ahead on the path she saw someone walking toward them, coming from the direction of the main building, not the other cabins.

Oh, hell. She grabbed Will's arm and dragged him off to the side, behind a tree.

"Why are we hiding?" he whispered.

"Shhh! Someone is coming."

As the figure got closer, she could see from the slight stature that the person was female and she wore a dark hooded jacket that hid her face. No member of the staff would have any reason for hiding her face. And as she got closer, Abi could see that she kept looking around, as if to make sure no one saw her.

Abi cursed under her breath. She was the right size, right height. It had to be Cindy.

And she had to put a stop to this now.

Abi waited until Cindy was almost parallel with the tree they stood behind, then stepped out in front of her.

Cindy let out a screech and stumbled backward, her hood slipping off her head, and Abi got her second shock for the night.

It wasn't Cindy sneaking to Tom's cabin. It was Claire—Noah's mother.

Chapter 15

"You don't believe her story about just being out for a walk?"

Abi looked over at Will sitting at the opposite end of the couch. "Of course not. I know exactly what she was doing. And I think she knows that I know."

"You don't suppose he's charging her?"

"Charging her for sex?"

He shrugged. "It's not unheard of. It happens at places like this. A kid needs extra money for college and the guests are willing to pay."

She dropped her head in her hands and groaned. This was awful. If something like that got around to the other guests and then to the public, it could be a disaster. "I'm going to have to fire him and I'm going to feel like the biggest hypocrite on the planet."

"You're not a hypocrite."

Oh, yes, she was. She'd never actually taken money for sex—that was a line even she wouldn't cross—but she had used it to manipulate men. What Tom was doing was really no different.

"I just don't get it," she said. "I talked to the director of the last resort he worked at. He has impeccable references. They *loved* him."

"Was it a woman, by any chance?"

She shot him a look. "That's terrible."

"But not unlikely."

He was right. She wondered how long this had been going on and if there were others. Brit had tried to warn her, and Abi should have believed her, trusted her. But she'd been too preoccupied with her personal life, too self-absorbed to care.

"Abi, can you really blame Claire? Her husband left her for a younger woman and she's about as angry and bitter as they come. Some good-looking *young* guy pays attention to her. Of course she's going to be interested. Hell, it might even be therapeutic. A little revenge goes a long way."

"That doesn't make it right. I'm going to have to tell Maureen. I can't help thinking this is my fault."

"Because of us, you mean?"

"Maybe he thought it was okay because I'm doing it." She felt like such a louse, even though she knew what she and Will were doing was different. They really cared about each other.

At least, she hoped he did.

"Abi, come here." He patted the cushion beside him

and she scooted over, cuddling against his chest. He folded his arms around her and kissed the top of her head. "You and I both know this is different. This is not about sex."

She rested her face against his chest, feeling his heart beat against her cheek. "What is it about then?"

He was quiet for several seconds, then asked, "Are you asking how I feel about you?"

"I—I guess I am. I don't want to push or rush you into anything. But I need to know if we have the possibility of some kind of future together. I need to know where this is going."

He sighed and rested his chin on the top of her head, stroking her hair back from her face, the way he always did. Already they'd formed habits, little things to show affection. Like a couple.

"I was convinced I would never get married again, but since I met you, everything has changed."

She looked up at him. "What are you saying?"

"What if I was wrong? What if I could be a good husband, a good father?"

"I think you would be," she said softly. "I think Adam does, too."

He smiled and touched her cheek, gazing into her eyes. "I want the chance to try, Abi. With you."

She let out a sigh of relief and hugged herself to his chest. "I do, too."

He wrapped his arms tightly around her. "I am so relieved to hear you say that."

"How will we do this? You live two thousand miles

away. I'm not sure if I could handle a long-distance relationship."

"The branch of government I work for has offices all over the country. I was thinking maybe I could get a transfer. Denver isn't too far from here."

Her heart rose up in her throat and tears burned in her eyes. "You would do that? For me?"

"Yeah, I would." He brushed his lips over hers, so soft and sweet. "I want to be with you, Abi. No matter what it takes."

"I want to be with you, too." She'd never wanted anything more, and nothing had ever felt as right as what they had together. "But there are things about me you don't know."

"What things?" he asked gently.

She pressed her face against the softness of Will's T-shirt so she would have to look him in the eye. If she saw disgust, she might not be able to handle it. "My mother took off when I was seventeen. I learned to take care of myself the only way I knew how. The way she taught me. I used sex to manipulate men. To survive."

Instead of being appalled, instead of pushing her away, he squeezed her tighter. He didn't speak. He just held her.

"I knew they were using me, too, but after a while I just…stopped feeling. I was dead inside."

"That's not you anymore," he said. "You have a good life and a beautiful son."

She smiled, the way she always did when she thought of Adam. "Everything changed when I found out I was pregnant. Everything that I'd done, it didn't matter anymore. And I knew that no matter what, I had to make a better life for my baby. I would do things differently. Adam means everything to me, Will."

"I know he does."

"I've done so many things I'm ashamed of, but I've changed."

"I know you have."

She should have known he would understand, that he wouldn't care. Maybe someday she would even tell him the rest. "I've never trusted a man before, but I trust you."

A stake driven through Will's heart couldn't have stung more or pierced deeper. Only then did he realize what he was doing getting involved with Abi. But it was too late. He was in too deep.

He loved her.

For the first time in his life he knew what a relationship was supposed to feel like.

Exactly what he felt with Abi.

It didn't matter what had brought him there, what she had done in the past, only that at this point in time they were both exactly where they were supposed to be.

He just hoped she would see it that way, too.

One more day. After tomorrow night, he would never have to lie to her again.

He stroked a hand across her cheek, then kissed her.

"Maybe since Adam isn't here we could go into my bedroom," she said.

"Abi, we don't have to." Though he loved kissing and touching her, couldn't wait to make love to her, what he felt for Abi was so much more than sexual. Just being with her was enough for now. "I don't want to do anything you're not ready for."

She rose from the couch, pulling him up with her. "We won't."

He grabbed his backpack from where he'd left it beside the couch and followed her into her bedroom. She flipped the switch by the door, and the lamp next to her bed turned on. She turned to face him, backing toward the bed. "Take off your shirt."

He dropped his pack on the floor and peeled his shirt up over his head. Abi did the same. She wore a lacy pink bra underneath. She reached back and unlatched it and tossed it on the floor with her shirt.

That night on the couch, it had been dark and he hadn't really seen her. He breasts were small and round, her hips full. She looked exactly as a woman was supposed to look.

"You're beautiful," he said.

She gazed down at herself. "I was thinner before Adam."

"You're perfect just the way you are."

She pulled back the covers and climbed in, scooting over to give him room. They lay side by side facing each other, as they had on the couch. Will pulled the sheet up over them.

"It doesn't bother you that I was with so many other men?" she asked, looking worried.

"You're with me now," he said, touching her face.

"There's so much we don't know about each other."

"We have time to learn. Abi, there is nothing you could say or do that would change the way I feel about you."

She could tell by the look in his eyes, by the sincerity in his tone, they weren't just sweet words to soften her up. He really meant it. Then Will kissed her, started touching her, and she stopped thinking about the past. She stopped thinking about everything but the tingly warmth where their bodies pressed together, the wet heat of his mouth as he kissed her lips, her throat, the ridge of her collarbone.

She unfastened his shorts, and he groaned as she slipped her hand inside his boxers. Like the rest of him, he was long and lean. She wrestled with the notion of sliding down under the covers and taking him into her mouth.

She was no stranger to pleasuring a man orally, but only because she knew it was what they liked, not because it was on her list of fun things to do. But the thought of doing it to Will, the thought of making him feel good, excited her.

At the same time there was something about what they were sharing, a feeling of innocence she didn't want to lose or corrupt. She didn't want to shatter the illusion that this was new and exciting and fresh. On so many levels it was.

In all the ways that counted.

Will needed no encouragement touching her this time. And he even managed to unfasten her shorts all by himself. He looked up at her and grinned when the button popped loose. But they were tighter than the pair she'd worn the other night, so even when he'd unzipped them he had a tough time getting his hand inside.

"Take them off," Abi said—ordered, really. Will wasn't used to taking orders from a woman, but he had to admit he was beginning to enjoy it. Especially when she was commanding him to get her naked.

He braced himself up on his elbow. "Are you sure?"

"I'm sure."

"Panties, too?"

She thought about it for a second, then nodded. "Everything."

"You're really sure? We don't have to rush this."

"Yes, *damn it*."

He hooked his fingers in the waist of her shorts and panties and eased them down very slowly, watching her face—the impatient, hungry look in her eyes. When he got them as far as her knees, she took over and kicked them the rest of the way down, to the foot of the bed, then wasted no time pulling his down, too.

They settled back down under the sheet, arms around each other, legs intertwined, bodies touching. He'd been naked with women before, many women—physically anyway. With Abi he felt stripped down to his soul. As they kissed and touched, explored one another, he knew that being with a woman had never felt this intimate. She found the ticklish spot on his right side, and he discovered a sensitive patch of skin on the back of her knee.

It sounded shallow as hell, but he'd never considered sex as anything but a way to reach physical gratification, to give his wives the illusion they were connecting somehow, to satisfy their emotional neediness, at least for a brief while. Fooling around with

Abi was…fun. And he was under the distinct impression she wasn't used to a man putting her needs ahead of his own. Every new place he touched or tasted elicited a gasp of surprise or a moan of pleasure. He took her to the brink over and over, backing off at the last second each time, and she did the same to him.

If this was a test of endurance, they would both come out winners.

"Will," she said, eyes heavy with desire. "Make love to me."

Something inside him said he should wait. They shouldn't take this any further, not until he told her the truth. But she was rubbing up against him, kissing him, and he was having a hell of a time telling her no.

"Abi—"

"If you ask me if I'm sure, I swear I'm going to kill you," she said through gritted teeth.

Ooookay.

She shoved him onto his back and rolled over him, straddling his thighs, and he knew he was a goner. She was going to take what she wanted and there wasn't much he could do to stop her. And he didn't want to. She leaned down and brushed her lips over his. "I have never been more sure of anything in my life."

If there had been any question before, any doubt that he loved her, he knew it now. This was what he wanted for the rest of his life.

"I need my pants," he said. She looked at him funny and he added, "Condom."

"Oh, right." She fished his shorts from under the covers at the foot of the bed.

He pulled his wallet from the back pocket, took out a condom, then dropped his pants and wallet on the floor. He was going to tear it open when Abi took it from him and ripped the packet with her teeth.

"Can I?" she asked.

Right, like he was going to tell her no. He'd never been one to gravitate toward aggressive women, but damn, he was really beginning to enjoy this. "Go for it."

He watched her as she rolled it on. He'd never seen anything more erotic, more beautiful, than Abi sitting there. He felt as if he'd been waiting his whole life for this.

"There hasn't been anyone since Adam," she said. "I'm going to take this slow."

Will nodded and wrapped his hands around the full softness of her hips to help guide her.

Inch by inch, eyes closed in concentration, Abi lowered herself on top of Will, then gasped as he stretched skin and muscle that had been neglected since Adam's birth. It felt like her first time, and maybe in her heart it was. The first time she'd made love anyway. All the times she'd had sex, she'd never felt like this, this complicated tangle of nerves and emotions.

She'd never felt anything at all.

When she sank as low as she could go, when they were joined completely, she stilled, letting her body get used to him. She looked down at Will to find him watching her.

Eyes locked, she lifted her body slowly up, then sank back down again, trembling as he touched even deeper inside her. Will sighed, and his grip on her hips tightened, his eyes never leaving her face. If she had expected pain, she'd been wrong. There was only pleasure. It came from somewhere deep inside her, a place she'd kept carefully guarded. Will was the key to unlock the door, and for the first time in her life she felt whole, alive. Everything that had happened before tonight, everything she'd done, no longer existed.

"Kiss me," Will said and she did. He tasted hot and sweet and he devoured her as if he was starving. She felt the world spin around her as their bodies tangled and locked, and when she opened her eyes she was on her back. He loved her slowly, sweetly, as if she were a delicate doll he was afraid he might break.

It wasn't enough.

Not even sure what she wanted but desperate for more, she writhed beneath him, wrapped herself around him. In response, he gave her what she wanted, what she needed, driving himself inside her. Her body spasmed and arched against him. He did it once more and she cried out. They moved together, hard and fast and deep. Bands of pleasure wrapped around her, squeezed and let go, and she shattered in Will's arms. In a haze she felt Will shudder, his body quaking with release.

She hadn't actually said the words yet, as if holding them in would protect her somehow, shelter her from the hurt if he didn't feel it, too. But she didn't need protecting any longer. "I love you, Will."

He looked down at her, brushed the hair back from her face as he so often did and smiled. "I love you, too."

Will switched on the lamp and looked down at Abi sprawled under the sheet, sleeping peacefully. He wanted to crawl back into bed with her, but it was time for him to leave. The sun was already rising, meaning he was going to have a tough time getting out of there without anyone seeing him.

He sat on the edge of the bed and touched her face. "Abi, wake up."

She didn't budge. The woman slept like the dead.

He gave her shoulder a gentle shake. "Come on, Abi, wake up. I have to go."

She groaned and muttered, "What time is it?"

"Almost seven."

She opened one eye and peered up at him, smiling sleepily. "Hi."

God, she was breathtaking. "Hi. I should go."

She groaned again and curled her hand into his T-shirt. "No, don't leave. I don't have to work until almost eight."

"It's getting light out. I should go before someone sees me."

"If you wait until after eight, all the staff will be gone and no one will see you."

She had a point. "You don't need time to get ready for work?"

"Ten minutes, tops. Which gives us plenty of time." She patted the bed beside her. "Climb in."

She didn't have to ask him twice. He pulled his T-shirt over his head and dropped it on the floor.

Abi yawned and drew one leg out from under the covers, threw her arms out and stretched.

That's when Will saw it.

The red heart-shaped birthmark at the top of her inner thigh.

Chapter 16

The clues had been there. She was the right age, the right height. Jesus, it even explained why she'd seemed like two different people at times. There'd been a dozen little things all screaming at him to take notice, and he'd ignored every one of them because he'd been too busy falling irresponsibly and stupidly in love with her.

Now there was no denying it. Abi was Crystal.

She gazed up at him, a puzzled look on her face. "Will?"

He looked at the mark on her thigh, then back up to her face. "It's you."

For a second she only stared at him, confused. Then the color drained from her face and her eyes went round with fear. For several long, oppressive seconds they only stared at one another. The air around them felt sticky and thick with tension. Then something came over her, a look in her eyes like he'd never seen before—the instinct to fight.

She pulled the sheet up around her and crept back against the headboard, looking like a tiger ready to pounce, but her voice was eerily calm. "Tell me you didn't know. That all this time you haven't been lying to me. Using me."

Will tried to swallow, but his mouth was dry. "I-I didn't know. I thought it was Maureen."

"I won't go back to Vince," she said, fear leaking into her tone, but she held her chin high. "You might as well kill me now. It won't be any worse than what he'll do to me."

"Kill you?" That's when he realized she thought Vince had sent him. She thought he was part of the Sardoni crime family. "Abi, Vince did not send me here. I'm FBI."

She inched farther away. "I don't believe you."

He reached for the backpack he'd left on the floor next to the bed, and Abi scrambled away from him. For all he knew, she had a weapon nearby, and he wasn't in the mood to be shot.

Will lifted both hands in front of him. "Relax. I'm not going to hurt you. I just need to get my identification from my backpack."

Very slowly, Abi watching him like a hawk, he bent down and unzipped the front compartment. He thought about grabbing his sidearm, but he didn't want to scare her. He eased his identification out and tossed it on the bed beside her. She picked up the leather case and flipped it open, then studied it for several seconds before she dropped it back on the bed.

"Do you have a weapon?" he asked.

"A weapon?"

"A gun."

"With Adam here? Of course not!"

"I just had to be sure."

She gathered the sheet more snugly around her. "I need to get dressed."

There was no way he was leaving her alone. He wouldn't risk her jumping out a window and taking off on him. He grabbed her shirt from the floor and handed it to her, then turned his back.

He could hear the covers rustling, movement on the bed. Then she said, "You can turn around."

She was still sitting on the bed, but she was dressed. "What are you doing here?"

"Looking for you. I've been searching for you for four years," he said.

"Why?"

"Ryan Thomas."

She looked confused, then awareness dawned in her eyes. "The agent Vince killed."

"He was my friend," Will said. "I was there when the car exploded. We were taking Gantz to testify."

"Your face." She held a trembling hand over her mouth. "Oh, God, that's when it happened. Vince did this to you."

"I should be dead, too, but I forgot my phone in the hotel room and went back to get it. It was dumb luck. I've been searching for you ever since."

"And you thought it was Maureen? All this time you've been using me to get to her, haven't you?"

Aw, *damn.* "Abi, it only started out that way, I swear. I wanted to become your friend in the hopes that it would get me in to see her. I never expected to feel this way about you."

"And I'm supposed to believe you? Your marriages—were those pretend, too?"

"The only thing I ever lied about is what I do for a living. Everything else is the truth. The way I feel about you is real."

"How did you find me? How did you even know where to look?"

"The call you made to Stephanie in Vegas last month. Because of her past involvement with the Sardonis, she's still being watched. It was a long shot, but I looked into it."

"I called her to see if he was still looking for me," she said. "She said that things had died down, that there was a rumor I was dead. I thought I was finally safe. That it was over."

"She was wrong."

"I don't understand. What do you want from me?"

"You gave us Vince. You were going to testify."

"That was *four* years ago."

"There is no statute of limitations on murder. I need you to come back to New York with me. I need you to testify."

She shook her head. "I couldn't then and I won't now."

"You'll be protected, relocated. You know it's the right thing to do. How can you turn your back on this?"

"My son, that's how."

"He'll be protected, too."

"You don't understand."

"I know you're worried that he'll be hurt—"

"Not hurt. *Stolen* from me."

"Stolen?"

"Will, don't you see? Adam is Vince's son."

He hadn't seen it coming. Abi could tell by the stunned look on his face that it had never crossed his mind. But she could see it sinking in now, taking hold, and she felt sick all the way down to her soul. Will hadn't even considered that he'd been forming a relationship with the son of the man who had killed his friend and scarred him for life.

It didn't get much worse than that. And though she understood the way he was feeling, it was completely unfair. Adam had done nothing wrong, yet he would pay for his father's sins. It was what she'd always feared. Why she'd tried so hard to keep him protected.

It was possible Vince may have been good to Adam, but he would have marked his son with the stigma of being the child of a hired killer. Abi just couldn't let that happen. Not then, not now.

"You told me Adam's father was dead."

"Are we going to start comparing lies, Will?"

He looked down and shook his head.

"Adam is the reason I disappeared. Why I never met with the agents. I would have done anything I could to send Vince to prison. Then I found out I was pregnant. I had to run. If I had stayed and testified, he would have

known and the family would never have left me alone.
They would have done everything in their power to take
Adam from me. I figured if it was just me, maybe they
wouldn't have looked so hard—eventually they would
forget about me."

"I'm going to ask you a question and I want you to
be completely honest with me. Did you take the hit
money?"

She didn't owe him an honest answer, but there was
no point in holding the truth in any longer. "I did it for
Adam. So he would always be taken care of. Vince
owed me that. Owed his son."

"You ran off with half a million in mob money and
you thought they would *forget* about you?"

"What would you have done? I had medical bills to
pay. I had to change my appearance."

"Change it how?"

"I had my breast implants taken out, my nose done,
a few moles removed. I guess I should have gotten rid
of the birthmark while I was at it. The rest of the money
is for Adam. For college. He's going to have a better
life than I did. Every advantage I never had."

"You didn't spend any of it?"

"Look around you, Will. Look at the way I'm living. Does it look like I spent a penny of that money on
my lifestyle?"

"Maureen knows who you are?"

"We met in Vegas years ago. She gave me a safe
place to stay, to raise Adam, until the heat died down."

"Then who is Maureen? And why is she hiding
here?"

"I can't tell you that."

"You don't have a choice."

His voice was so cold she nearly shivered. This was a darker, more intimidating side of Will that she'd never seen. And he was right—she was in no position to bargain. He held all the cards here. He was in control. "You have to promise not to tell anyone. If it gets out that she's here, that she owns this place, they'll never leave her alone."

"Who?"

"The press. The public."

"If she's done nothing illegal, I don't have to tell anyone anything."

"Maureen's real name is Cara Black."

"Cara Black? The *singer?*"

After years of being in the tabloids, going through four divorces and half a dozen stays in rehab battling drug addiction, everyone knew who she was. Cara had decided the only way to heal, to make her life right, was to disappear from the public eye. "We met in Vegas years ago, long before I met Vince. When I ran from Vince, she was the first person I called. I knew she would help me. We take care of each other. If it gets out that she owns this place, it will be swamped by the press. I don't know what that will do to her. She's been clean for almost four years now, but she's still fragile. She would never admit it, but the thought of being discovered scares her to death."

"I won't tell anyone who she is. But, Abi, you have to come back with me. You have to testify. Until Vince is behind bars, you'll never be safe."

"Vince could be dead and it wouldn't be over. Not as long as I have his son."

Will sat on the edge of the bed. "No one has to know. He'll be kept in protective custody until after the trial. After that you'll be put in witness security. Get a new identity."

"That could take months."

"But he would be kept safe."

She shook her head. "No. Absolutely not. I won't leave my son with strangers."

"Abi, you may not have a choice. Someone may have followed me here."

Her heart slid down into her stomach. "What did you say?"

He explained how someone had been tailing him. How Will had been following her to make sure she was safe.

"All this time you've been following me? Watching me? It's why you wanted to hike with me, isn't it? It's why you always seemed to be around?" She didn't know if she should punch him or thank him. She felt so violated and at the same time grateful he'd been protecting her. "That means they may already know about Adam."

"If they knew it was you, they would have taken you by now. I'm convinced they think it's Maureen."

"Who?" she asked. "Who is it?"

"I don't know. I ran everyone's name. All the guests. Everyone checked out."

And what if they figured out the truth, that it was her? "I have to get out of here. I have to go before they figure out who I am." She got up, looking frantically around, suddenly unable to think, to remember where she'd put her duffel bag. She could only pack as much as she could carry. Just a few things for her and Adam.

Will stood, too. "Let me call my boss. We'll make arrangements to get you and Adam out of here and no one will know. Abi, I need you to testify. I need you to make this right."

"Will, I can't help you. You know how these people work. Odds are, I won't ever see a witness stand."

"Then why were you going to do it before?"

"When I met Vince, I didn't know who he was. By the time I figured it out, he owned me. I was afraid to leave. Then I saw that agent's wife and kids on the news and I realized Vince had killed him. I knew I had to turn him in to make up for the way I'd lived, for all the horrible things I'd done. If I was killed, at least I would have tried. But now I have Adam. He needs me. I can't take the chance."

"I won't let you leave."

"*You* don't have a choice."

"You admitted you took the money. I don't know that you weren't involved. I can take you into custody for questioning and you could be charged with accessory. You would lose Adam anyway."

"You would do that after you said you love me?"

"I do love you, but this is not about you and me. I have a job to do. And you have a responsibility to make things right."

Abi could feel her heart splitting in half. Her legs felt wobbly, and she sat down on the edge of the mattress, dropping her head in her hands. Either way she was screwed. Either way her son would grow up without her. If she went to prison and Vince found out he had a son, he would get custody of Adam.

She wanted to hate Will for what he was doing to her, but it wasn't him. He was only doing his job. She had done this to herself. Would she spend the rest of her life paying for her sins?

Will sat down beside her. "In the four years since you left he's killed eight people, Abi, and those are just the ones we're sure of. Eight more murders, and who knows how may others, that will go unpunished. We have to stop him."

She rubbed the heels of her palms into her eyes. She was so tired of this, so tired of the guilt, of being scared someone would find them. She used to think someday it would end, but she recognized now it would *never* be over. As long as Vince was walking free, he would always be looking. And killing more innocent people.

She realized Maureen was right. It was time to stop hiding, to do the right thing and face her past. It was the only way.

She looked up at Will. "You promise you can keep Adam safe."

Every part of Will sighed with relief. He didn't want to have to arrest her, take her son away. In fact, he wasn't even sure he could have done it. If she had grabbed her son and run, he might not have had the heart to stop her. "He'll be safe."

"You have to swear that if something happens to me, Vince will never get custody of Adam."

"Nothing is going to happen to you."

"You have to *promise* me."

"I promise."

"Then I'll do it," she said. "I'll testify."

"Here's what we're going to do. I'm going to call my boss and let him know I'm bringing you in. You're going to pack a few things for you and Adam, enough to fit in your backpack. If we walk out of here carrying luggage, whoever has been watching me will know something is up. We're going to get Adam from Maureen and drive to the field office in Denver. The arrangements should be made by then, and we'll get you on a flight to New York."

"Did you mean what you said about transferring out here to be with me? Would you really have done that for me?"

"Abi—"

"I know it's over, Will. You have a career and a life. You can't go into hiding just because I've screwed up my life. I just need to know if you really would have done it. If you were telling me the truth."

"I would have."

She nodded, tears rolling down her cheeks. She felt sick. Sick and alone in her heart and in her soul. She'd brushed happiness with the tips of her fingers, held it in her hand for a few brief hours, and now it had slipped away.

Will touched her shoulder, but she shrugged off his fingers and stood up, wiping her face with the back of her hand. If it was over, then it had to be over for good. "I should pack. And I have to talk to Maureen, tell her what happened. I have to figure out a way to explain it to Adam."

Will knew she was right. There was no way to make this thing between them work. It had to end. Knowing that didn't make it hurt any less. And it did hurt, more than any pain he'd ever experienced.

But right now he had a job to do, a woman and her child to keep safe.

He unclipped his phone from his belt, but the battery was dead. "I need to use your phone."

She was stuffing clothes into her backpack. "Fine."

He grabbed his backpack off the floor and reached inside, where he kept his sidearm. "Dammit."

Abi turned to him. "What's wrong?"

He felt around, but it wasn't there. His gun—their only protection—was gone. And he knew exactly what had happened. Last night, when they'd gone to see Tom, Will had left his backpack in her cabin.

He cursed under his breath. How could he have been so careless?

Out of the corner of his eye he saw movement by the bedroom door, and his heart sank.

"Looking for this?"

Chapter 17

"*Eric?*" Abi said. "What are you doing?"

He stood in the bedroom doorway holding Will's gun. Now it all made sense why Will couldn't pin down who'd been following them. He'd run all the adults' names, but he'd never thought to check out the kids. But he was guessing Eric was no kid. His name probably wasn't Eric, either.

"Mikey," he corrected and gave Abi a greasy smile. "It's Crystal, right? Vince is going to be real happy to see you."

This was Will's fault. He should have known, should have figured it out. "The resort will be swarming with agents in about five minutes," he said, hoping he could bluff his way out of this.

"Nice try. But I heard everything. I know you didn't put the call in yet."

"Don't do this," Abi said. "You're so young. You don't have to be like them. Nothing good will come of it."

Mikey turned to her. "If it makes you feel any better, I felt bad when I found out it was you. You were okay. But Vince is family. And speaking of family, isn't he going to be surprised when he finds out he's a daddy?"

All the color drained from her face. She looked so pale Will was afraid she might pass out. It was very important they both stay conscious and aware if they were going to get out of this alive.

"You're going to pick up the phone," Mikey told Abi. "You're going to tell Susie you're too sick to work. You're going ask her to have me pick Adam up."

She shook her head. "No way."

Mikey raised the gun, pointing it at Will's head. "How do you think this bedroom wall is gonna look with your boyfriend's brains all over it?"

Will could see by the cold, dead look in his eyes that he would do it. He may look like a kid, but he had the heart of a killer.

Abi looked over at Will and he shook his head. At least if Mikey shot him, someone could hear the blast and call the police. As long as Mikey didn't have Adam, they would have some leverage. "Don't do it."

Mikey walked toward Will, gun pointed at his head, finger on the trigger, an evil smile on his face. "You know I'm gonna enjoy this."

"I'll do it," Abi said.

"Abi don't."

She picked up the phone and dialed. "I won't be responsible for your death, too."

What she didn't understand was he was already dead. There was no way Vince would leave any witnesses. Especially an FBI agent. Especially him. He had no weapon, no backup, no plan.

Abi's voice was unnaturally calm as she told Susie she wouldn't be working today and Eric was picking up Adam. Now it might be at least a day before someone figured out that she was gone. She would probably be dead by then.

"Good girl," Mikey said when she hung up the phone and then he turned to Will. "You've got cuffs in the bag. Take them out and put them on the bed."

Will pulled them from his pack and tossed them on the rumpled covers where he and Abi had spent half the night making love. If there was any way to get out of this, any way to survive, he wasn't letting Abi go again. He didn't care what it took—they would make it work.

Mikey grabbed the cuffs and stuffed them into the back pocket of his jeans. "These will come in handy later." He motioned them toward the door. "C'mon. We're going for a walk."

He led them out the door and behind the cabin, into the woods, following the tree line at the base of the mountain. Will knew where they were headed; he'd memorized every inch of the grounds. Mikey was taking them to the road off the service entrance at the back of the retreat, where Vince was most likely wait-

ing and no one would see them or think to look if they
suspected anything was amiss.

The air was hot and felt thick in his lungs. Sweat
soaked his T-shirt, molding it to his skin. In the distance
he could hear voices, the sounds of the retreat waking,
but they were far away and getting farther with every
step they took.

He had to do something.

Abi walked silently beside him; Mikey kept a safe
distance back. He may have been young, but he wasn't
stupid. If Will had any hope of getting the gun away
from him, he needed him closer.

"I want you to pretend to twist your ankle," Will
whispered to Abi.

"What for?" she whispered back.

"I need to get him closer. I'm going to try to disarm
him. When I grab him, run to the nearest building as fast
as you can. And do not look back, no matter what you
hear."

"He might kill you."

"Yes, but he won't kill you. Vince would have ordered him not to. Abi, it's your only chance."

She shook her head, tears rolling down her cheeks.
"I won't do it. I won't let him kill you."

"Do you really think Vince is going to let me live?
You might be able to get away. You could call the police."

"The police are twenty minutes from here."

"Abi—" he protested.

"Knock it off, you two," Mikey warned.

Damn it, why wouldn't she listen?

Several minutes later the trees thinned and he could see the service road ahead and the outline of a dark car parked there.

"Almost there," Mikey said, sounding as excited as a kid getting a new toy.

The sun was blinding as they emerged from the dim light of the forest, and Will might have used that to his advantage, but it was too late.

They were standing face-to-face with Vince Collucci.

Vince stood by the black Cadillac, wearing an Italian silk suit, arms folded across his chest. He was still physically beautiful—no one could deny that. It was part of his mystique, what had drawn her to him. But on the inside he was dark and ugly.

He had no soul.

Abi should have been terrified, but all she felt was numb, dead inside. She could only hope that Vince would kill her quickly. She hoped he would take good care of Adam. She wanted to hope that he wouldn't kill Will, but she knew that was too much to ask for.

Though she'd never really believed in God or an afterlife, maybe if there was one, she would see him there.

"I can see why you didn't recognize her," Vince told Mikey. He pushed off the car and walked slowly toward Abi, looking her up and down. "She does look different. I can't say it's been an improvement, though."

If he thought his words would hurt her, he was wasting his time. She'd rather be the homeliest woman in the world if it meant being beautiful on the inside.

"Baby," Vince said in that honey-sweet voice that still haunted her dreams, "did you really think you could hide from me?"

"I managed for four years, didn't I?"

His smile slipped and something dark and dangerous flickered in his eyes.

"She's got a surprise for you. Don't you, Crystal?" As if Mikey couldn't wait for her to break the good news, he took it upon himself. "You've got a son, Vince."

Vince's expression went from dark to explosive. "What?"

"Yeah, he's a cute kid, too," Mikey said. "She raised him good."

Vince pulled a gun from under his jacket and advanced toward her, but Will stepped in his path.

"Don't try to be a hero," Vince said. "Not when you're the one that led us here in the first place. We've been doing this dance for four years, Bishop. I guess I won."

Will's voice was cold as ice. "Not yet you haven't."

In her peripheral vision Abi saw Mikey raise his gun and aim it at Will's head.

"Come here, baby. Come to Vince."

If she didn't, they would kill him. She stepped out from behind Will. Will made a move to grab her, and Mikey clocked him on the back of the head. He grunted and went down hard on his knees.

Though her first instinct was to help him, she knew it would only make things worse. When Vince gave an order, he expected it followed.

Swallowing the terror that was building inside her, she forced her legs to carry her to where Vince stood.

He stared at her with those cold, dead eyes. "You stole my money *and* my child?"

She met his stare with her chin held high. She wouldn't give him the satisfaction of seeing her fear. He thrived off it.

"He's with the other kids at the retreat," Mikey said. "As soon as we take care of Bishop, I'll go get him."

Vince grabbed her by her hair, and she winced as he spun her around, pulled her back against his chest. "You'll never steal from me again," he breathed in her ear. "I'm going to make you suffer for this."

Bile rose up her throat. So much for quick and painless.

"Where is it?" Vince hissed, pressing the butt of his gun to her temple. "Where is my money?"

It figured that he cared more about finding his money than seeing his son. "Somewhere you'll never find it."

"You'll tell us." The grip on her hair tightened, pulling her head back. "Mikey tells me you and Bishop were going at it pretty hot and heavy last night. I see some things don't change. Now you get to see him die."

She looked down at Will, on his hands and knees, still disoriented from the blow to his head. Vince took the gun from her head and aimed it at Will, and her heart slammed against the wall of her chest. "I've been looking forward to this for a long time. Say goodbye, sweetheart."

It happened so fast, Abi wasn't sure the exact se-

quence of events. One second Will was on the ground,
stunned, the next he'd produced a knife from out of nowhere and stabbed Mikey in the leg. Mikey screamed
and his gun discharged. Then his body jerked, as if he'd
been punched, and he collapsed on top of Will. Behind
her Vince fired, then jerked, his grip on her hair loos-
ening as he fell to the ground. Then there were people
everywhere, appearing from the woods surrounding
the road—men wearing jackets that said FBI.

Where had they come from?

Abi looked around, stunned.

One of the agents grabbed her and pulled her away
from Vince's body. "Are you injured?"

"N-no," she said.

"Agent down!" someone shouted, and for a second
Abi was confused, then she looked over to where Will
lay. They pulled Mikey off him and she saw it. The
blood. So much blood, all over the front of his shirt,
soaking the thigh of his shorts. An agent knelt beside
him, applying pressure to the left side of his chest.

Abi heard a scream, then realized it had come from
her.

Abi sat on Maureen's couch, her hands shaking so
badly she could barely grip the cup of tea someone had
handed her. Every time she closed her eyes, all she
could see was the blood. And when she thought of Will
lying there helpless, she felt sick inside.

Adam lay curled up beside her, taking a nap, sacked
out from all the commotion. He'd been more excited
and curious than frightened by all the men with guns,

by the atmosphere of panic when he and the rest of the guests had been herded into the main building until the area was secure. He'd asked about Will a couple dozen times already, and she'd managed to avoid the subject and distract him.

Four hours had passed and she still didn't know if Will was dead or alive. There had been *so much* blood. She had tried to get to him, to help him, but the agents had dragged her away, said they had to keep her safe, in case there were more of them.

The man that had introduced himself as Agent Robbins, Will's immediate boss, was standing near the kitchen, cell phone to his ear. She'd been trying to get them to tell her something about Will. Anything. But no one was talking.

She knew she and Will were finished, that whatever they'd had was over. She just needed to know that he was okay.

One thing she did know was that there would be no trial, no need for her to testify. Vince was dead. So was Mikey. And no one else had been with them, meaning her secret was safe, no one in the family would find out about Adam. That didn't mean she was out of the woods. When word got out Vince had been killed and he'd found her, the family would be looking.

Later that night she and her son would be taken to a secure location and held there while arrangements were made for her new identity. It was the least they could do considering they'd blown her cover. And she'd handed over the key for the safe-deposit box where she'd been keeping the hit money. That part of her life wouldn't truly be over until that money was gone. She wasn't sure how she would get by, how she would care for Adam, but she would figure out a way.

Maureen sat beside her. "Can I get you anything, honey?"

Abi shook her head. "I can't stop thinking about him, wondering if he's okay. I need to know that he's all right."

"I'm sure he will be."

"I should hate him for lying to me, for using me, but I don't. I still love him." She looked over at Maureen. "Why do I still love him?"

"Maybe if he loves you, too—"

"No. There are no maybes. I'm being relocated. He has a life. It wasn't meant to be." She looked around at the agents, the commotion. "God, I'm so sorry about this."

"It's okay."

"If your name gets out—"

"Abi, it's *okay*. I'll deal with it. We both knew there were risks, right? It was good while it lasted. And who knows? If my name doesn't get out, maybe this will be good for business."

"Ms. Sullivan?" Agent Robbins said.

She turned to him, her heart skipping a beat. Maybe he had information about Will. "Yes?"

"I just wanted to let you know we'll have you out of here tonight. In a little while someone will escort you to your cabin to pack. Only the things you'll need to get by. The rest will be held in storage until you're relocated."

She let out the breath she'd been holding. "And my new identity?"

"It can take several weeks. You'll be safe until then."

"I was wondering.... Will never got the chance to call you. How did you know Vince was here?"

"We've had someone on Vince since Agent Bishop got here. When Vince moved, we followed him."

In other words, Will had been bait. She wondered if he knew. "If you knew Vince was coming after us, why didn't you stop him?"

"We had to wait until he made a move. I tried to call Agent Bishop, but he wasn't answering the phone in his room or his cell."

"He was with me, in my cabin. And his cell phone battery was dead." If he had only gone back to his cabin last night, if she hadn't asked him to make love to her, he would never have been shot.

"And what about when Vince had us on the road?" she said, her voice rising. "Why did you wait for them to shoot Will?"

"Vince got there about two minutes before you. We had to get our snipers in place." He laid a hand on her shoulder. "It was all last-minute. We did our best."

Robbins's cell phone chirped and he answered it. He was quiet for a minute, then asked, "Agent Bishop?"

Her heart leaped up into her throat. *Please,* please *let him be okay.*

"I understand. I'll take care of it." He clipped the phone on his belt and turned to her.

She looked at him hopefully, but he shook his head.

"He never regained consciousness. I'm sorry."

It took several seconds for his words to sink in, for the tears to well up and choke her. Then pain squeezed so tightly around her heart she couldn't breathe.

Will was gone. And it was all her fault.

Chapter 18

"We're almost there."

Abi looked out the car window at the passing scenery. She'd never been to Wyoming before, nor had she ever thought she would want to live there, but it was pretty enough. Rough and rugged but peaceful and secluded. She could get used to this. She hadn't even known until they'd crossed the state line where they were going. But they'd heeded her request that her new home be located in the mountains. At this point, she didn't care where it was as long as it wasn't a third-rate hotel.

The past four weeks had been the longest, most miserable of her life. The agents assigned to her wouldn't let her so much as walk to the ice machine alone, and

Adam was used to being outdoors, being with other children. He'd grown tired of the television within the first two days. He'd driven her and the agents half-crazy with his whining and complaining. She'd tried to be cheerful and keep his spirits up, but it was tough when her heart was broken. And every time he asked about Will, if they would ever see him again, another piece of her heart chipped away until she feared soon there would be nothing left. She didn't tell him much, only that like the other retreat guests, Will had gone home.

After two weeks Adam had finally stopped asking. He seemed to forget. She only wished she could, too. But Will haunted her in her dreams. In her sleep he would come to her and hold her and tell her everything was going to be okay, it was all a mistake, he wasn't really dead. She could feel him and smell him. She would wake with her pillow wet and a pain so deep she wanted to go back to sleep and never wake up.

Will had given his life for her. He'd saved her. She couldn't help thinking that if she'd only testified four years ago, this never would have happened. All those people Vince had killed would still be alive. She wished she could get one more chance to see him, one more opportunity to tell him despite everything that had happened she still loved him. And she probably always would.

She would never meet another man like him.

The SUV pulled off the road and bumped up a gravel driveway.

"We're here," Agent Rodriguez told Adam, who sat with his nose glued to the window, having called out his millionth "Are we there yet?" of the trip not two miles back.

Both Rodriguez and Agent Roth were childless, and Abi didn't doubt that after the past four weeks with Adam, they would remain that way for a very long time—possibly forever.

"We're there, Mommy! *Look!*" Adam screeched, bouncing in his seat. The kid was so filled with pent-up energy he was about to pop.

They pulled up in front of a small cottage-style house with green shutters and overgrown flower beds. It definitely had potential. But she couldn't muster any real enthusiasm. Maureen, all of her friends at the re-treat—she would never see them again. It was good to be starting over—it was what she needed—but she felt inexplicably lonely. No one would ever know who she really was, just the cardboard-cutout identity the FBI had given her.

When the car rolled to a stop, everyone got out and stretched. Agent Rodriguez grabbed her bags while Roth went up and unlocked the door. "Nicole," he said, holding it open for her.

For a second she wondered who he was talking to, then realized it was her. She still wasn't used to her new name. All of this was going to be an adjustment.

She stepped inside her new home and turned slowly

around. It was small and cozy and looked to be in decent shape. There was a family room, a small kitchen to
the back and, to the right, an arch that she suspected led
to the bedrooms and bath. All of their things had already
been delivered. She'd expected she would have a fair
amount of unpacking to do, but there were no boxes. In
fact, it looked as if everything had already been unpacked.

Adam darted past her to find his bedroom. Unlike
her, he'd been so excited to see their new home. He'd
kept asking her if there would be other kids, if he would
have new friends. For the first time in his life he would
make friends that wouldn't leave after several weeks.
This would be so good for him.

"All the information you need is in the packet we
gave you," Roth told her. "Your new ID, social-secu-
rity card."

"Got it," she said. She walked into the kitchen and
opened cupboard doors. They were filled with her
dishes and stocked with food. Coincidentally many
were Adam's favorite treats—all new and unopened.
Someone must have taken inventory of her cabinets at
the retreat. It was more than she would have ever expected from the government.

"If you don't need anything else, we're going to
take off," Rodriguez said.

"Thank you," she told them both. They probably
couldn't wait to be rid of her. "I appreciate all you've
done for us. I know it wasn't fun most of the time."

"Good luck." Roth flashed her a smile and then they

were gone. The entire miserable ordeal was, for the most part, over.

"Mommy, Mommy!" Adam hopped excitedly in the archway. "Come see my room! It's just like home."

She grabbed the bags containing their clothes and toiletries and followed him to the door on the right.

"See, Mommy! All my stuff is here!"

She peered inside, then gasped and dropped the bags at her feet. The room was set up nearly identically to his bedroom at the retreat. The bed and dresser and shelves—they were arranged precisely the same. Not only that, there were things she'd never seen before— new toys, like a foam football and a baseball with a glove small enough for his little hand.

She went down the hall, past the small bathroom, to her bedroom. Tears burned her eyes. It was a little bigger than her place at the retreat, but like Adam's room it was set up nearly the same. The furniture was in the same place—even the lamp and clock were on the nightstand on the left side. And like the other rooms, there were no boxes, nothing to unpack. She opened the closet and found her things hanging there.

This was too weird. Who would go to all the trouble to do this?

From the other room she heard a knock at the door. Probably one of the agents had forgotten to give her something. She would ask them to thank whomever had gone to such lengths to make their new house familiar and comfortable.

She walked to the living room and pulled open the door—

She froze. For several seconds she couldn't breathe, couldn't think, just stood there too stunned to move. She had to be dreaming or hallucinating. It looked like him, but…

This couldn't be real.

"Will!" Adam shrieked.

"Hey, sport." Will crouched down in the doorway, and Adam barreled past her to launch himself into Will's arms. Will hugged him hard. "Boy, did I miss you."

"Me, too! Mommy said you went home and we wouldn't see you again."

Will stood, Adam clinging to him, and flashed her that crooked grin. "Mommies make mistakes sometimes, I guess."

She nodded numbly. He looked paler, maybe a little thin. But his face…

Adam laid a hand on his cheek. "What happened to your scar?"

"It's called a skin graft," Will told him. "They took the bad skin off and put new skin on. Looks pretty good, huh?"

Adam nodded enthusiastically.

There were still scars where they had grafted the new skin on, but his face looked almost normal. So different. "I thought— They said you were—" she began.

Reality hit her with the velocity of an express train and a sob ripped from her throat. He wasn't dead. All this time he'd been alive.

He set Adam down and pulled her into his arms,

held her against him. The scent of him, the feel of his body—it was really him.

"I'm so sorry," he said. "But they couldn't tell you."

"The bullet wounds—there was so much blood."

"I bled like crazy, but both bullets managed to miss any major arteries."

"The reports on the news, the memorial service in New York—"

"All staged. It had to look real if I was going to go into the program."

She looked up at him, tears streaming down her cheeks. "Program?"

"Witness security."

"Witness security? You mean you—"

He stepped back and held out a hand for her to shake. "Jack Traynor. Pleased to meet you."

She looked at his hand, her knees feeling weak and shaky. "You left the FBI? For me?"

"Yep."

"Your whole life?"

"Uh-huh. Everything. As far as anyone knows, William Bishop is dead."

"I don't believe it. No one has ever made that kind of sacrifice for me."

He took her face in his hands, grinned down at her. "If I hadn't left the FBI, hadn't had the chance to spend the rest of my life with you, *that* would have been a sacrifice."

"Hey!" Adam tugged on the leg of Jack's pants, a frown on his face. "Your name's not Jack. It's Will."

"He got a new name, honey. Just like Mommy used

to be Abi and now she's Nicole. So from now on you have to call him Jack."

"How come? I like his old name."

Jack knelt beside him. "Kinda confusing, isn't it?"

Adam nodded.

"Maybe it would be easier if you just called me Daddy."

Adam's eyes lit with excitement. "Really? Could I?"

"If it's okay with your mom." He looked up at her. "What do you think? Is it okay if he calls me Daddy?"

She nodded, a new round of tears rolling down her face. He stood and pulled her into his arms again.

"When I thought you were dead, it tore me apart," she said. "I love you so much."

"I love you, too. I want us to get married and be a family."

"I want that, too."

"Hey," Adam said, tugging on Jack's pants again. "Since I have a daddy now and you love Mommy and you're gonna get married, does that mean she can have a baby?"

Jack grinned. "Sounds okay to me, sport. What do you think, Nicole?"

"A baby?" she said, gaping at the two of them, her head still reeling. "You don't think we're getting a little bit ahead of ourselves?"

"You don't want any more kids?"

"Well, yes, of course I do. Could we maybe get married *first,* then talk about a family?"

Jack looked down at Adam. "Your mom has a point.

We probably should get married first." He grinned at Nicole. "I'm free Saturday. How about you?"

She couldn't hold back a smile. Five minutes ago she'd been miserable and lonely and suddenly she had her entire life ahead of her—life with the man she loved. Maybe her past was finally where it belonged—in the past. It was time to move on for good, and considering it was Friday, they weren't wasting any time. "Saturday works for me, too."

"So we get married and then Adam can have a little brother or sister?"

"A brother," Adam said. "Girls are gross."

"Sorry, pal," Jack said with a shrug. "We can't make any promises. You sort of get what you get."

Adam thought about that for a minute, then sighed. "I guess a girl would be okay, as long as she doesn't touch my toys."

"Well?" Jack asked her.

"Okay," Nicole agreed.

"Hooray!" Adam bounced around the room. "When can we get it, Mommy?"

"Well," she told him, "the baby needs time to grow, and sometimes it doesn't happen right away. Sometimes it takes, um…practice."

Adam looked puzzled. "Can't you start practicing now?"

She and Jack shared a smile—one that said they'd start as soon as Adam went to bed.

"Sport," Jack told him, "we'll get right on it."

Then Jack gave her a kiss, slow and deep and sweet, just the way he always did.

"I can't believe you're really here," she murmured.

"I'm really here."

"It was you that unpacked our things? Got the house ready? You did all this?"

"I wanted you to feel like you were coming home."

Nicole looked around at her new house, at her son so happy and healthy, at the man who had given up everything because he loved her so much.

Loved *her*.

She smiled up at him. "I've definitely come home."

* * * * *

If you enjoyed OUT OF SIGHT,
you'll love Michelle Celmer's next book,
HOUSE CALLS, available from
Silhouette Desire in January 2006.

INTIMATE MOMENTS™

**They'd die for the people they love.
Here's hoping they don't have to....**

The Sheriff of
Heartbreak County

Available January 2006
Intimate Moments #1400

When a congressman's son is murdered,
all fingers point to Mary Owen, mousy
newcomer to Hartsville, Montana, but
Sheriff Roan Harley isn't sure. At first his
interest is strictly professional—but where
will the lawman's loyalties lie when he
realizes he's in love with his suspect?

Available at your favorite retail outlet.

SPOTLIGHT

The only thing they have in common is a killer...

USA TODAY bestselling author

MARIE FERRARELLA

SUNDAYS ARE FOR MURDER

FBI agent Charlotte Dow is on the hunt for her sister's murderer and finds herself frustrated, yet attracted to Nick DuCane. Together they must battle the mind of a psychopath, as well as their own personal demons, to put a serial killer away.

"Marie Ferrarella is a charming storyteller who will steal your heart away."
—*Romantic Times*

A dramatic new story coming in January.

Where love comes alive™

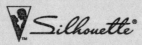

COMING NEXT MONTH

#1399 PENNY SUE GOT LUCKY—Beverly Barton
The Protectors
When an eccentric millionaire leaves her riches to her beloved dog, Lucky, girl-next-door Penny Sue Paine is assigned as his guardian. But someone wants this pooch dead…and fast. Enter Vic Noble, gorgeous ex-CIA operative hired as Lucky's protector. Suddenly Penny Sue starts thinking *she's* the one who got lucky!

#1400 THE SHERIFF OF HEARTBREAK COUNTY—Kathleen Creighton
Starrs of the West
A congressman's son is murdered and all fingers point to Mary Owen, the mousy newcomer to Hartsville, Montana… but Sheriff Roan Harley can't quite make the pieces fit. At first he's interested in Mary for purely investigative reasons. But where will the lawman's loyalties lie when he realizes he's in love with the suspected criminal?

#1401 AWAKEN TO DANGER—Catherine Mann
Wingmen Warriors
Nikki Price's world comes crashing to a halt when she wakes next to a dead body. Added to this ordeal is the man sent to solve this mystery, Squadron Commander Carson Hunt, who broke her heart months ago. Carson is certain she's in danger and vows to protect her. Will Nikki be able to trust Carson with her life…and the passion threatening to consume them?

#1402 ENEMY HUSBAND—Nina Bruhns
FBI agent Kansas Hawthorne won't rest until the criminal that betrayed her father is brought to justice. Only her archrival, Stewart Rio, a tough-as-nails agent, could make her falter on this top secret operation. Posing as newlyweds, their pretend romance turns to real love. Will their new relationship survive the past so they can have a future together?

SIMCNM1205

INTIMATE MOMENTS